Young Nathan

B-43

Young Nathan

MARION MARSH BROWN

Decorated by Don McDonough

THE WESTMINSTER PRESS

Philadelphia

1993

1993

To My Husband
*who inspired me
to write this book
and*
To My Son
for whom it was written

Contents

CHAPTER 1

A New Epoch

DUSK WAS falling early, and Nathan, stopping for the dozenth time at the kitchen window to peer down the darkening lane, wondered if he should light one of the tallow candles he and Enoch had molded the night before.

" I wish they'd come," he said aloud and turned to two small pinafored figures who were busily fencing off the imaginary fields of an imaginary farm in front of the fireplace. " You'd best pick up your pebbles. Pa said they'd be home before dark, so they ought to be here any minute. We want everything shipshape for *her!* "

He glanced about the room again to see if anything had been left undone. The hearth was clean, the wide boards of the floor were scrubbed white, and the small panes of the windows shone. An appetizing smell of meat and onions came from the big black pot that hung over the fire.

Nathan had been up since dawn, marshaling his little army of younger brothers and sisters in an attack on the dust and cobwebs and disorder that simply would descend upon the twelve big, low-ceilinged rooms of their home. Enoch and John, the two older boys, had been in the fields cutting corn for the stock. Work had been exciting that day, for it was an eventful day in the lives of the ten young Hales.

" What do you reckon she'll be like? " asked Joanna, looking up from her pile of pebbles.

"I think she'll be pretty," said Nathan, " and she won't be serious all the time like pa. She'll laugh and sing — " He broke off suddenly as the two little girls gazed eagerly at him. He was frightened — for them, and for himself, and for his brothers. What if he were wrong?

But he had no more time to think about it, for the outside door had burst open.

" They're here! They're here! " shouted Sammy, dumping a load of wood into the woodbin with a crash. " Nathan, they're here! "

Falling over each other in their haste and excitement, three other little boys scampered in.

" We saw her," Joe panted. " She only comes to pa's shoulder."

Nathan frantically pushed in shirttails and tried to smooth tousled hair. " Where are Enoch and John? "

" Doing chores."

Then quiet descended. The door had opened again, and Deacon Hale stood before them, tall and angular, with a fair-haired woman at his side.

" This is your new mother," he said to the children. " Abigail, these are the children: Nathan — "

Nathan stole a quick glance at his stepmother's face and sighed in relief. He bowed as his Grandmother

Strong had taught him. " We — we're glad you're here," he said.

She was not so young as he had expected her to be, but there were little laugh wrinkles about her eyes, and she looked pretty with her cheeks pink from the wind and with little curls blown about her face.

" — and Elizabeth and Joanna," the Deacon went on, naming the children in the order in which they stood ranged before him, "and Samuel and Joseph and Billy and David and Richard — "

His father sounded like the teacher calling roll on the first day of school, Nathan thought in sudden amusement.

" Nathan, where are John and Enoch? " the Deacon asked.

" Doing chores, pa," Nathan answered. He turned to Abigail. " The girls will show you the way upstairs. I — I thought — I mean, I hope you will find everything all right." The sentence ended in confusion.

" I'm sure I shall." Abigail's eyes smiled at him.

Joanna skipped to her side and caught her hand. " This way," the little girl beamed. " I know everything's all right, 'cause Nathan made everybody work all day gettin' things fixed up for you."

Nathan flushed as Abigail turned back from the door.

" That was splendid of Nathan," she said. " It's going to be wonderful having a big boy who's so thoughtful. I have a big girl, who will soon be here, but it will be ever so much fun to have a whole tribe of boys — and two *little* girls! " She smiled at the serious-eyed row of little boys and at the two girls at her side. " My Alice must be about your age, Nathan. She's a good little housekeeper, but she couldn't have done better than you have."

Nathan flushed again, embarrassed but pleased.

" Thank you, ma'am," he said, shifting self-consciously from one foot to the other.

Abigail and Joanna started up the stairs, with Elizabeth walking shyly a few steps behind them. The door closed on Joanna's chatter, and the sound turned the three spellbound, statuesque little boys, standing speechless in the middle of the floor, into jumping jacks. They grabbed their caps and leaped for the door, throwing it wide to the screeching wind.

Nathan and his father were left alone in the big old kitchen that was full of shadows thrown by the flickering fire.

" Well, son, you had best get the candles lighted," the Deacon said gravely. " I'll go out and unhitch Old Nell. Never leave a good horse standing out in a chill wind after she's been driven. Remember that, son."

" Yes, pa," Nathan replied. But it was of women, not of horses, that he was thinking, and of what a difference they made in a place. The house had seemed like a home again the minute his father's new wife had stepped inside the door. No, he had not been wrong about her. They would all be happy and gay together. Under his breath, he said a little prayer of thanks.

He stooped to stir the kettle of stew simmering over the flames, and the bright light of the fire shining on his face disclosed fine features, alert, intelligent eyes, and a chin of strength and determination that was like his father's.

He looked up from the kettle to the plate bearing the family coat of arms which hung above the mantel — three broad arrows, feathered white, on a field of red. The white feathers must stand for purity, but the red — He wasn't sure about that.

" Probably it's for courage," Nathan said to himself as he continued to stir the stew. He must ask his father about the Hale ancestors who had lived under that coat of arms. Had they done any great deeds? he wondered. And even more, what might he and Enoch and his other brothers do in the future to live up to the coat of arms? He smiled at the thought of any of them having any special courage. Hadn't they all been scared as rabbits over their stepmother's arrival today? He ladled out a spoonful of the stew, blew on it for a moment, and licked the spoon hungrily.

" I wish they'd hurry for supper," he said aloud.

CHAPTER 2

Advent of Alice

NATHAN SLIPPED into the quiet kitchen where Abigail was rolling out crusts for six deep pumpkin pies for Sunday dinner. She had been with them two months now, and already Nathan found he could scarcely remember what life had been without her. His stepmother looked up as Nathan entered but did not speak. Staring at the toes of his shoes, he broke the silence.

"Pa says he wants me to go after Alice."

"He told me he was thinking of sending you."

"He says he needs Enoch and John to clean out the barn," Nathan said unhappily.

"Don't you want to go?" Abigail asked in surprise. "I thought you'd be glad of the chance to see Reverend Huntington."

Nathan looked up then, his eyes alight. "I could take my propositions in to him. They're all finished!" Reverend Huntington was tutoring him for Yale. "But I don't know much about girls," he added, downhearted again; "only Joanna and Elizabeth, and they're just my sisters."

Abigail rubbed her chin, getting a smudge of flour on it.

" Alice will be one of your sisters, too."

" The trouble is I won't know what to talk to her about — or — or — "

" Alice isn't hard to talk to," Abigail said reassuringly. " She'll have you laughing before you're out of Jeff's store where you're to meet her."

" But how'll I know her? "

" I have no doubt she'll be the only girl waiting in the store, and she'll be wearing a red hood. She has black curls and merry, laughing eyes."

Nathan sighed and pulled on his boots, then started winding about his neck the red muffler Abigail had knit for him. She had also made one for Enoch, for she said the boys needed them, riding in to Reverend Huntington's each week to be tutored.

Yale seemed very remote to Nathan, though he and Enoch were to enter the following year. But he enjoyed his studies, especially mathematics, and was anxious to get into trigonometry, which Enoch was studying. Enoch should have started to Yale this year, but the Deacon thought it would be best for his two sons to go together, so that each could act as a check upon the other. Nathan was sorry Enoch had to wait for him, for his brother was intent upon becoming a minister and was anxious to start his preparation. John, on the other hand, was not interested in going to college. He wanted to be a farmer, and Nathan knew he would be a good one.

" Well," he sighed, not being able to prolong his preparations, " I guess I'll be starting."

" Don't forget the groceries," Abigail said.

Nathan felt in his pocket for the list. As he climbed

on Old Nell's back, he had a terrifying thought. How would he get Alice on the horse? He had seen men in town become lost in a billow of skirts as they lifted their wives or daughters onto their horses. Suppose he dropped her?

Bending his head against the wind, he decided to think of more pleasant things. He liked nothing better when alone than to imagine himself one of the people he read about in his history books. Today he became Oliver Cromwell, putting old, fat King Charles on trial for the wrongs he had done his subjects.

In his imagination, he heard the people pleading with him: " You'll be struck dead if you raise a hand against the king. Kings are divinely appointed by God to rule." And his reply: " That is only a superstition. You must be free of it before you can taste of liberty! "

Carried away by his dream, he did not realize he had reached the village of Coventry until the mare stopped at the Reverend Huntington's hitching post.

Nathan slid down off the horse's back. Old Nell will be ready for college by the time Enoch and I are, he thought wryly.

He was disappointed when there was no answer to his knock. He had been anxious to leave his propositions with his tutor and get another set.

Without direction, Old Nell moved on to the general store. Nathan dismounted and stood looking in the window at a conglomerate assortment of heavy work shoes, harness, printed calico, chewing tobacco, and coffee beans. Finally he gained sufficient courage to turn toward the door. He pursed his lips into a soundless whistle and attempted what he hoped was a non-chalant saunter up the steps.

Suddenly the door opened, and Jeff called heartily: " Hello, there! Been alookin' fer ye."

Nathan stumbled and only saved himself from falling by catching at the door.

" There's a young lady awaitin' fer ye," Jeff told him.

In a far corner of the room Nathan saw a patch of red. It came toward him.

" Oh, I'm so glad you're here! " Alice cried. " I thought you would never come."

" I'm s-sorry if I've kept you waiting," Nathan stammered, embarrassed by his undignified entrance.

" It's just that I'm so anxious to see ma," Alice explained.

Of course she would be, Nathan thought.

" I'm glad you're coming to live with us," he said, suddenly ashamed of his reluctance to come for her. " As soon as I get these things — " He gave Jeff the list.

Alice was at the window. " Is that your horse? "

" Yes," Nathan replied. " Her name's Old Nell, and she's as slow as molasses in January." It's just like her ma said, he thought. She's as easy as can be to talk to.

" I'll go out and get on," she said, opening the door.

Nathan sighed in relief. Old Jeff set the groceries on the counter and Nathan stowed them in the knapsack on his back and picked up the gray canvas " telescope " which held Alice's clothes.

Alice was behind the saddle, her legs spraddled across the mare's broad back. Nathan mounted and caught the reins with his left hand, held out the

" telescope " stiffly with his right.

Alice started to laugh. " Give that to me! " she commanded. " Your arm would break, holding it like
that."

Instead of handing it to her, Nathan fastened its
strap to the saddle horn.

" That's better," Alice said, still laughing. Nathan
liked her laugh. He had a good, warm feeling inside
him as he turned the mare toward home.

" Oh, this is fun! " Alice cried, as Old Nell got under way, lurching from side to side with every step.

Before it seemed possible to Nathan that they could
be home, the big white house, with wide brick chimneys at either end and a long, sloping roof between,
appeared on top of the next hill.

" That's your new home," he told Alice.

There was sudden pride in his voice. The Hale farm
was the best in all the countryside, and it was wonderful that Alice was coming to live there with them.
Smoke curled up from the chimneys. Nathan thought
of the cheerful kitchen and the savory odor of Abigail's
baking. He kicked his heels against the horse's fat sides,
trying to hurry her.

That night supper around the long kitchen table
took on a festive air. Even Enoch, who was usually
slow to smile, laughed at Alice's gay chatter. But Deacon Hale regarded the merrymaking seriously. At
length he said to Alice in his stern way, " I hope, my
dear, that you will grow up to be as fine a woman as
your mother."

Nathan stole a glance at the girl and felt a choking

resentment against his father, for the light of Alice's happiness seemed to have dimmed as if a cloak had been thrown over it.

I'll tell her, as soon as I get a chance, not to be scared of pa, he thought — that it's only his way.

He did not want to see Alice's gay spirits dampened. There had been so little gaiety around the old Hale farm.

CHAPTER 3

Off to College

ALICE SNIPPED off the gray yarn with her even, white teeth, slipped the one remaining stitch from her knitting needle, and pulled through it the short little tail of yarn she had left dangling.

" There," she sighed, lying back against the straw-stack which protected her from the wind and from any curious eyes of big or little Hales. She watched a fleecy white cloud change from a puffy mushroom into a galloping white horse, and planned how she would tuck this pair of socks into the pocket of Nathan's coat with a note: " Nathan, I made these especially for you. Love, Alice."

She had knit other socks for Nathan and some for Enoch, had taken turns with her mother and stepsisters at the spinning wheel, and had stitched busily with them on clothes for the boys to take with them to Yale. But this pair of socks was different, a special gift for Nathan.

September was here, and in the morning Nathan and Enoch would set out on horseback to ride the sixty miles to college. Alice knew that she would miss both of the boys, but it was of Nathan she thought as she idled briefly before going back to the bustle of preparation in the house. She would miss the long tramps she and Nathan took together in the woods, his little jokes, and his happy whistle.

The sound of the familiar whistle made her jump up and stuff her knitting into the big patch pocket on her apron. Nathan was coming toward the stack, carrying a bucketful of water from the well.

" Look, Alice! I can do it," he cried exultantly.

" Do what? "

" Swing the bucket in a circle over my head without spilling a drop. I'll show you."

Alice jumped back as the pail started to swing. Then she gave a gasp, for the bucketful of water had come down squarely on Nathan's head.

" All right, laugh," Nathan said sheepishly. " I'll show you yet." He started back toward the well.

" Don't! " Alice begged. " I'll take your word for it."

" I'm not going off to college without showing you I can do it," he vowed. In a few minutes he was back with another bucket of water.

Alice held her breath. Up — over — down went the bucket. Not a drop of water had spilled.

" Nathan, you did it! " she cried in delight. " Now you'd better get into some dry clothes," she added practically.

" Then will you meet me at our secret nook? " he asked.

" I have to gather the eggs," she replied uncertainly. From the nook at the end of the pasture lane they had often watched the clouds and listened to the birdcalls in the woods beyond. But Alice felt that today would not be as other days. This would be their last time alone together for ever so long. When Nathan returned from college, things might not be the same. She wanted very much to do as he asked, yet was reluctant without knowing why.

"I'll help you gather the eggs when we get back," he promised.

"All right," she agreed, and went to the kitchen for the egg pail.

"Whatever are you doing?" she asked Elizabeth, who stood by the table tying pots and pans together with strips of cloth.

"Fixing these so the boys can carry them," Elizabeth replied. Abigail was wiping salt off the outside of a ham. When the Reverend Huntington had gone to Yale, students did their own cooking. So Nathan and Enoch were going prepared.

"I'll gather the eggs," Alice said, feeling a little prick of guilt. She ran down the path to the barn and left her bucket. The secret nook was not far away, lying just over a grassy knoll that shut it off from view of the house. The other three sides of the nook were screened by hazel bushes. Nathan had shared its seclusion with her since her first day on the farm.

She slid over the knoll into the grass-carpeted bowl. Nathan stretched out his hands and caught her.

"I wanted to see you alone before I left," he said.

There was a queer little ache in Alice's throat. She

did not look at him for fear he would notice the tears in her eyes.

" Alice, will you write to me while I'm at Yale? "

Alice looked up in surprise. " Letters? " she asked. Letters were so rare that the arrival of one always frightened her. Once or twice a year someone riding by from Boston stopped at the farm to leave a letter from the Deacon's brother. The bearer was fed and kept overnight. A letter was something to think of with awe.

" You will, won't you? " Nathan urged.

" How would I get them to you? " Alice asked doubtfully.

" Your mother will send clothes and things to us when someone's going our way. You could slip a letter into a pocket."

Alice's eyes were suddenly teasing. " What if Enoch should find it? " she asked.

" I wouldn't give him a chance. I'd get at the things first." And then Nathan was smiling, for he knew that she would write.

" I have to get back and gather the eggs," she said.

" You — you won't forget me when I'm gone? "

She shook her head and they walked toward the barn.

" You'll have an awfully good time at college," she finally managed to say.

" I guess," Nathan replied. " But I'll miss everything here — especially you."

They gathered the eggs, and Alice turned toward the house.

" Good-by, Nathan." There was a queer little gulp in

the middle of her words.

" Good-by, Alice," Nathan replied, very low.

She ran toward the house. Once she looked back. Nathan was standing in the shadow of the barn, his hands in his pockets.

" Alice," Enoch's voice called to her from the big lilac bushes at the corner of the back fence. " I've been waiting for you." He was smiling his slow smile.

Alice stopped, startled. " You frightened me, Enoch."

" I'm sorry. I only wanted to tell you good-by when the others weren't around."

Alice was secretly a little amused. First Nathan, now Enoch. She was fond of Enoch. He had been a good brother to her.

" Good-by, Enoch. I hope you'll be very happy at Yale. I know you will, because you'll be studying for the ministry, and that's what you want more than anything else in the world, isn't it? "

" That, and one thing more."

" What's that? " she asked in surprise.

" I'll tell you some other time," he said after a moment. " You're in a hurry now."

" Oh, yes! " she cried, remembering that she had been a long time gathering the eggs. Enoch unlatched the gate, and she hurried through.

Bedtime was always early in the Hale household, for the Deacon saw to it that everyone was up at dawn ready for a full day's work. There was seldom a break in the toil except for church, or an occasional spelling bee or singing school. The boys' departure for college had the family at such a pitch that sleep seemed hopeless. But even earlier than usual the Deacon began to wind the big clock on the mantel.

Reluctantly, Alice went upstairs. She had already tucked the special pair of socks and the note for Nathan into the pocket of his coat. It seemed that surely she could not sleep.

But the next thing she knew, the Deacon's lusty voice was calling the boys to get up. She sprang out of bed and into her clothes.

The sun had not yet risen when the big breakfast of fried potatoes, ham and eggs, baked beans, and apple pie was over. Alice, with the others, crowded about the boys as they loaded their horses. She half smiled, there in the semidarkness, when the Deacon said: " Rest your horses often, boys. Remember, they're good horses and good horses should always have the best of care."

Nothing came ahead of his horses with the Deacon, Alice thought — not even his sons.

Then she felt the quick pressure of Nathan's fingers on her own.

" Come on, Enoch," he said. " Let's get started."

The boys mounted.

" Good-by, boys," said Abigail. " I know Yale will be proud of you someday."

" Just live as you've been taught, my sons," the Deacon was saying, " as God-fearing, upright men. You know right from wrong. Be sure you always follow the path of right. Don't forget your prayers, and remember that ' straight is the gate, and narrow is the way, which leadeth unto life, and few there be that find it.' " He gripped his sons' hands.

There was a chorus of good-bys, the clomp-clomp of the horses' hoofs. Alice stood waving after the two dusky figures as they disappeared down the lane. Nathan was riding behind, and she felt sure that she saw him turn and wave as the horses rounded the hedge at the end of the lane.

CHAPTER 4

Brick Row

" HALE SECUNDUS! " came a shout from down the hall. Nathan grimaced, hastily marked the line of Hebrew he was trying to translate, and made for the door.

" Yes, sir," he called as he reached the hall.

" Come here."

" Coming," Nathan answered, starting on a run toward the room from which the order had issued. He had learned to respond quickly when an upperclassman spoke. He pushed open the door of a room identical with his own except that where his had been quiet and unfogged, this one was filled with the lively discussion of several upperclassmen and the dense smoke from their pipes.

The wall of smoke made Nathan cough. " Why," he began, " don't you raise a — " Then, remembering that he was only a freshman, he broke off.

" What's that you said? " boomed a senior named Rowe, who was seated near the door.

" Nothing," Nathan replied innocently. " What was it you fellows wanted? "

" We want to know what you started to say, Freshie,

and no evasions," replied William Hull, a sophomore whom Nathan greatly admired, and who was to become one of the new country's versatile statesmen.

Nathan tried to look cheerful. He had learned that taking with a smile the hazings imposed by the upperclassmen worked to one's advantage.

"Well, I started to say, ' Why doesn't somebody open a window in here before you choke on the smoke? ' but I decided I wasn't the one to make the suggestion."

"Your hind thought was better than your forethought, but it came a little too late," Rowe said wryly. "What'll his penalty be, fellows? "

"Send him for our tobacco," a voice called, "and we'll figure it out while he's gone."

"Right! Hale Secundus, we want you to go to Benedict Arnold's shop in Crown Street and bring us a canister of tobacco, and don't waste any time. When you get back you will pay your penalty for impertinence."

"Yes, sir." Nathan bowed and waited.

"Well, what are you waiting for? " a sophomore yelled. "Can't you see my pipe's out? "

"Some money, if you please, sir," Nathan replied.

"Money? What's the matter with the money in your own pocket? Isn't it good in New Haven? "

"I have only a few pennies, sirs, not enough to buy a canister of tobacco." Nathan and Enoch had soon discovered that it did not pay to have more than a few pennies in their pockets, for the upperclassmen seemed to consider a freshman's money their good luck. And the Hale boys knew that every penny their father had given them would have to be accounted for before they received more.

"Where's Hale Primus?" someone demanded. "Does he carry the pocketbook for the Hales?"

"I don't know where my brother is, sir," Nathan replied. "He wasn't in his room when I came from class."

"Here," Hull said, pulling out a coin and tossing it across the room. "This'll do it."

"Thank you, sir." Nathan turned from the room quickly before they could think of further errands.

Once outside the new brick dormitory in which he lived, he set out at a lope for town — past the old frame dormitory, painted a disturbing sky blue, and past the one other college building, a brick chapel with a great clockface in its tower.

Nathan glanced at the clock and saw that it was almost four. He had wanted to complete his Hebrew translation before supper, which was served at five. He and Enoch had soon learned that cooking their meals was no longer necessary at Yale, for meals were now served in the Common. The Hebrew would just have to wait, for some kind of session would certainly be awaiting him when he returned.

As he turned into Crown Street, a voice hailed him from the door of a little bookstore.

"Ho-ho, Hale! A mighty senior after you?" It was his roommate, Gridley.

"Not yet," Nathan replied, slowing down, "but there will be if I don't get back in a hurry with tobacco."

"Going to Arnold's? I'll go along with you. I've been buying myself a pony."

"A what?" Nathan asked in astonishment.

"Oh, not one to ride!" Gridley laughed. "At least

not one to ride about the country. Just one to ride through Virgil."

Nathan laughed, recalling the new meaning for the word " pony " that he had learned since coming to Yale. They reached the apothecary shop, and Gridley looked up at the sign above the door.

" Good, isn't it? " he asked. " ' *Sibi Totique.*' I don't need a pony to translate that."

" ' Wholly for himself,' " Nathan said. " That's the way Enoch and I translated it the night we rode into town."

" So does everybody else — except Arnold," Gridley grinned. " He says he meant it to read, ' For himself and for all.' "

Benedict Arnold, a dark, handsome young man, was behind the counter. After they had purchased the tobacco, the two boys walked briskly back to Connecticut Hall.

" Well, good luck," Gridley said as he stopped at the room he and Nathan shared.

" Thanks," Nathan answered, his imagination working on what fate awaited him down the hall. A roar of laughter came from the room as he approached. He was not afraid, despite the fact that he was only fourteen years old. It was his age and Enoch's that had earned them the nicknames " Hale Primus " and " Hale Secundus."

" Here's your tobacco, sirs," he said at the door.

A chorus of shouts answered him:

" Throw it here."

" Give it to me if you know what's good for you."

Nathan, hesitating only the fraction of a second, tossed the tobacco to Hull. Hull was a friend, even if he was an upperclassman.

" Thanks," Hull rewarded him.

Nathan waited as the tobacco was passed from hand to hand and tipped into one pipe after another. He had never smoked, and he watched with some curiosity; but chiefly he was impatient to be off. However, he knew it would never do for him to depart, pretending to have forgotten that he had a penalty coming, nor to ask for the verdict.

Finally, when the pipes had been lighted all around, Rowe ran his hand over his hair thoughtfully.

" Where's your pipe, Hale Secundus? " he asked. " We might give you a pipeful of our tobacco for going after it."

The room came to sudden attention, like a schoolroom when the teacher enters.

" Thank you, sir, but I don't smoke," Nathan answered, sensing something back of this seeming generosity.

At once, voices broke out again.

" Now's the time."

" He'll never learn any younger."

Nathan saw clearly what was coming. He wondered if he should have tried smoking at home where there was a chance for a fellow to go out behind the barn alone. He remembered the time he and Enoch had come upon their brother John leaning weakly against the barn door, a sickly pea-green color.

Now everyone was offering him a pipe.

" Try mine," Hull said.

" No, mine," Rowe insisted.

Nathan was the center of a circle of extended arms. He swallowed and tried to appear unconcerned.

Rowe scratched his head. " I'll tell you what. I've an old briar here that gave me my start. It comes in handy now and then. Our friend, Hale Secundus, shall make its acquaintance. It's good and strong."

Exclamations of approval filled the room. The pipe was produced and filled.

" Now, Hale Secundus," said Rowe, " right here in the center of the room. We'll give you instructions. There's nothing difficult about learning something new if you have a good teacher."

Nathan started to seat himself cross-legged on the floor.

" Oh, no," Rowe interrupted. " I — " he cleared his throat. " I think you will be able to follow our directions much better if you remain standing."

Obediently, Nathan stood.

" Now, here's the pipe."

Nathan took it awkwardly.

" You hold it like this — " Rowe tapped a coal from his own pipe into Nathan's. " Now, pull on it."

Nathan put the stem into his mouth.

" Pull. Got it? "

Nathan shook his head. The pipe had a nasty taste.

" Here! Another coal, somebody. You've got to learn to get a light, Secundus. That's lesson number one."

Uproarious laughter followed. Nathan tried again, and coughed as the first acrid puff went down his throat. Automatically, he removed the pipe from his mouth with a grimace of distaste.

"Keep it in!" voices yelled at him. Nathan put the pipe back into his mouth, swallowed to alleviate the sharp stinging in his throat, and tried again. He choked, clamped his teeth down on the stem, and sucked more gently. The coal in his pipe glowed, and he glowed a little himself. But what did you do with the smoke? You couldn't swallow it. When he drew it into his lungs, it burned and choked him. Shouts greeted his efforts.

"Keep her going."

"Don't take it out."

Hull was lolling on the bed, his pipe between his teeth, but his face seemed blurred and his figure weaved before Nathan's eyes. The furniture began to reel, and involuntarily Nathan glanced toward the window, which was still tightly closed.

"Aha!" he heard someone exclaim. "The pea-green tinge."

"Keep it up, Secundus. Keep puffing."

He closed his eyes and puffed. Perhaps it wouldn't be so bad if he couldn't see things whirling around.

"His legs won't hold him much longer," he heard, and tried to grip the floor with his toes. Not for the world would he fall with all these fellows looking on and jeering. If only that overpowering nausea would leave!

Then the familiar sound of the clanging supper bell cut through his misery. If only they would leave him! He opened his eyes to see if they were going, but shut them again quickly at the sickening way his stomach lurched.

"Somebody's got to stay with him to see that he smokes the pipeful."

It seemed to Nathan that the voice came from a long way off. He almost staggered for the window.

"I'll stay," a voice said. The voice was Hull's. That made matters worse. To have Hull see him —

The noise died away as the hazers trooped out, calling back admonitions to Hull to see that their victim should "smoke that pipeful to the last grain."

"It's all right, old fellow." Hull's arm was about Nathan, supporting him. "Just let me help you to your room. I'll smoke the pipeful out. They'll never know the difference."

Nathan leaned against Hull and let himself be led, keeping his eyes closed against the advancing and receding walls of the hall.

"There," Hull said. "Just lie still awhile, and you'll feel better. Want me to pull your boots off?"

Nathan only wanted him to get away — out of the room, quickly.

"No, please, sir," he managed to say. "Thanks."

The door closed, and he reached frantically for the bucket which stood under the washstand near by.

Nathan was awakened by Gridley shaking his shoulder. Outside the window lay darkness. He wondered dully what time of night it was.

"Wake up, wake up, Nathan," Gridley was saying. "You'll be late for chapel. It's a quarter past five. I overslept."

Nathan groaned as Gridley threw back the covers and lighted a candle. The whole sickening experience of the night before swept over him.

" Guess they made you pay kind of heavy, didn't they? " Gridley asked.

" Plenty," Nathan replied. " But at least I got home before I disgraced myself completely."

" And you smoked the whole pipeful!" Gridley exclaimed admiringly. " That's what I call showing them. The first time I tried to smoke, three puffs did me in."

Nathan struggled into his trousers. So Hull had really let them think he had finished the pipe. That was being a friend! Wait till he got to be a sophomore; maybe he could chum with Hull.

" Come on," Gridley urged. " We've got only three minutes to get into our seats in chapel if we don't want to be late for roll call."

" And that I don't! " Nathan responded emphatically, trailing after his roommate.

The day was a long one, for it was misery for Nathan to go to classes unprepared as he was forced to do that day. To make matters worse, it was Friday, and on Friday six members of the class were always called upon for declamations in Latin, Greek, or Hebrew. He sat hunched miserably in his seat, knowing it might well be his turn. But the minutes of the first hour ticked away, and then the second, and still the gray-haired professor had not called his name from the classbook.

Nathan heaved a sigh of relief when the class was over. Outside he found Enoch waiting for him on the steps, looking extraordinarily vivacious.

"Great news," Enoch cried. "Reverend Fry was here today. He spent night before last at Coventry. He brought us provisions and letters." Mr. Fry was an itinerant preacher — a friend of the Deacon, who often spent a night at the Hale farm when passing that way.

Nathan's heart skipped a beat. This was the first time they had received any communication from home since Christmas time, when the Deacon had sent them a turkey, and a note saying that he hoped they would observe the season devoutly and that all were well at home. Nathan had been keenly disappointed by the absence of a letter from Alice then, but he had felt sure it was because she had found no opportunity for sending one. But this time she would surely have found a way.

"Where are the things?" he asked in excitement.

"In my room. I haven't had time to see what's there. I just got out of class. President Daggett sent a message to me that Reverend Fry had brought a bundle."

The boys hastened down Brick Row to Connecticut Hall and up the stairs.

"Hear the boys were a bit harsh with you last night," Enoch remarked, glancing critically at his younger brother. "You look a little peaked today."

Nathan flushed, but he did not resent his brother's patronizing tone. He knew Enoch was a little jealous of him because he was quicker at his studies and also better at sports.

"Ha!" Enoch cried, as they entered the room and caught sight of the bundle on the bed. "I'll venture there's some good eating in that as well as some new socks."

Nathan made a dive for the package. Neither food nor clothing interested him at the moment, although he liked to eat and was fastidious about his dress. His chief concern was to discover if Alice had been able to send him a letter. He went through the contents of the bundle rapidly, tossing things to Enoch after making sure there was no message in them.

" Socks," he reported, hitting Enoch in the stomach with a roll of them. " And new mufflers. Guess those will keep our chins warm."

" Wonder who knitted the mufflers," Enoch mused. Nathan did not reply. He had found what he was looking for.

" Letters," he said. " One from father, and one that says ' Enoch,' and another that says ' Nathan.' " Surely that round girlish hand would be Alice's. He felt a keen disappointment that she had also written to Enoch. It couldn't be Elizabeth's writing, could it? He turned toward the window with his letter, unfolded it with fingers that were not quite steady, and glanced hastily at the signature. It was " Alice." He perched himself on the table to read.

" It's from Alice!" Enoch exclaimed, as he opened his letter.

" H'm," Nathan mumbled. A happy quiet filled the room as he forgot Enoch and read:

Dear Nathan,

I miss you so much. I never go to our secret nook any more. It makes me lonesome. I wanted to write you the other time, but I didn't have a chance. I hope you are having a good time and are not forgetting us all.

When are you coming home for a vacation? I have tried and tried to swing a bucketful of water over my head without spilling any, but I can't — not even with a little bucket. Old Spot had twin calves. I guess that's all the news. Alice.

Nathan reread the message and glanced up to find Enoch still engrossed in his.

" What does she say in *your* letter, Enoch? "

" About the same as yours, I suppose. Let's see what pa has to say." Enoch unfolded another sheet addressed to both of them.

" ' Dear Boys,' " he read aloud, " ' I hope you remember that you are at college to learn, and that you are attending to your duties. Remember that the price of more than one good horse is going into your education. Make good use of your time. We are well and hope you are the same. Pa.' "

Nathan laughed. " Pa never forgets his horseflesh," he commented.

CHAPTER 5

Home-coming

THERE WAS only a band of light in the west as Enoch and Nathan turned their horses' heads into the lane that led up to the big white house that was home. They had been away from it for a year, and Nathan's pulse quickened with the horses' steps as the familiar landscape of low, rolling hills, and the house with its face turned toward them, came into view. " I will lift up mine eyes unto the hills, from whence cometh my help." Nathan always thought of that verse in connection with the house. It symbolized the people living in it too, for they were of simple faith, living close to the earth, loving God's hills and valleys, lifting up their eyes.

Nathan looked toward the orchard back of the house, a blur of darkness now. But he knew exactly how it would look in the morning with the sun shining on it. Bright red apples would dot the thick green foliage on branches bending low with the weight of ripening fruit. He breathed deeply and caught the delicious, spicy odor of apples on the evening air.

With Enoch beside him, he rode up the lane in silence, deeply touched by this first home-coming. Suddenly the silence was shattered by an exciting, recurring yell like an Indian war cry. Little David had caught sight of the horses. His cry brought feet running from all directions.

Nathan saw Abigail framed in the light of the doorway and thought that she represented all the strength and beauty of womanhood. Another picture flashed quickly into the doorway and was gone. He caught his breath at how much Alice had grown to look like her mother. She had changed in a year from a little girl to a woman.

Pandemonium had broken loose by the time the horses reached the hitching posts in front of the house. Each of the younger boys was trying to be the first to greet the brothers from college. But it was Joanna, grown taller, but still chubby, who reached Nathan first, got him around the legs as he swung down off his horse, and was hoisted to his shoulder. Then into the confusion came the dignity of the Deacon as he strode in from the barn, followed by John.

It was a gala evening in the Hale farmhouse. Everyone talked at once, and as they talked, Nathan's eyes and thoughts wandered to Alice, crouched with Elizabeth in front of the fireplace, roasting chestnuts for a homecoming treat. Her cheeks, flushed from the heat of the fire, were as red as the apples in the basket at her side, and her eyes, shining with excitement, were the blue of midnight skies.

But what Nathan dwelt on was what he read in her face. She loved life, just as he did, reaching out her hands for it eagerly and happily. Merry and fun-loving as she was, however, she was not lightheaded and ir-responsible like the girls in New Haven who ogled the boys from Brick Row. Her laugh, as it rang out at something Enoch had said, bubbled up as naturally and joyously as the water in the pasture spring.

There was a loud knock, and the talk stopped short as the Deacon strode to the door. An evening visitor was rare among the Connecticut farmers, for they worked hard and long and were usually ready for bed when their late supper was over.

" Good evenin', Deacon," a pleasant, boyish voice said at the door. " I heard the boys got home, and I had to be the first to git over an' see 'em."

Enoch and Nathan were on their feet in an instant, slapping the visitor on the back and wringing his hand.

" How have things been since we left, Asher? " Enoch asked.

" My, but it's good to see you! " Nathan exclaimed.

Asher Wright had been born three weeks before Nathan on the farm below the Hales'. Since babyhood the boys had played and worked together.

" Come on over by the fire, Asher," Abigail invited, " and try some of the chestnuts the girls have been roasting."

The babble of excited, happy talk burst forth again.

" What's this here goin' to college like? " Asher asked curiously. The Hale brothers had been part of a life that he knew he would never experience and had no desire to experience, but he did wonder about it.

" Oh, it's fine! " Nathan replied with enthusiasm. " We live in two dormitories — sixty of us — "

" Sixty boys all agoin' to college? " Asher asked in amazement. He had visualized a class of eight or ten boys, tutored by a man who looked and talked like the Reverend Huntington.

" Sixty of us right now. Of course, Enoch and I don't see much of most of the fellows. There are just a few of us who get together to talk and study, to go rowing or walking, or to run races. There's my roommate Gridley, and Wyllys, and Tallmadge — he's a fine fellow; he can write poetry like anything."

" Poetry? " Alice breathed. " You mean one of the boys you know writes poetry? "

" Yes," Nathan replied. " It just rolls off his pen. And there's Robinson, and Hillhouse, and Alden — all good fellows."

" Are they God-fearing, prayerful men? " the Deacon asked.

" We're all prayerful," Nathan said mischievously. " We have to be in chapel for prayers at four thirty every morning in summer, and at five thirty every morning in winter."

" What better place could you be, my son? " the Deacon asked.

Nathan saw Alice's face cloud at his father's reproach.

" I meant no disrespect," he said quickly.

" We want to join a literary society next year," Enoch said, just as quickly.

" What's that? A lit-lit-lit-er-ary society? " Asher wanted to know.

" A group of fellows that get together to have debates and discussions," Nathan explained.

Finally, much later than usual, the Deacon yawned, took out his big watch, and said, "Time for bed." Even then everyone was loath to leave the fireside.

"John and I are in the last haying," the Deacon told his returned sons. "I guess you'd best help us finish with it tomorrow. Then you can start picking apples."

Reluctantly, the children dragged off to bed. David was asleep on the floor by the fireplace, and Nathan stooped to pick him up. As he lifted him, he found himself face to face with the plate bearing the Hale coat of arms. He stood looking at it, holding the sleeping child in his arms.

"What are you looking at, Nathan?" Alice asked, pausing before she ascended the stairs.

"The old coat of arms."

"And what are you thinking?"

"How I used to dream about what I could do some-day to live up to it," he said with a wry smile. He started toward the stairs. "Thanks," he said, "for writing me that letter."

Alice flushed. "It wasn't anything," she answered, dropping her eyes. "I — I wrote one to Enoch too."

"Yes, I know."

"Ma knew I was writing, so I thought —"

"Of course," Nathan said.

He carried David up the stairs, smiling happily to himself in the darkness.

In the days that followed Nathan gloried in his strength as he lifted great forkfuls of sweet-smelling hay to the wagon.

"You've developed muscle," his father said, noting

the ease with which he pitched the hay, " and you've grown taller."

" I'm six feet now," Nathan boasted.

" We Hales are six-foot men," the Deacon nodded. Then in an altered tone, " Enoch tells me you aren't sure you're going into the ministry."

Nathan hesitated. " Why, I — "

" It's your calling, son," the Deacon said. " You've got the gift, like your grandfather before you. People will follow you."

Nathan thrilled at this unwonted praise from his father, even though the subject disconcerted him.

" Enoch's so sure," he tried to explain, " and I'm not. It isn't that I don't want to do good in the world — " His voice trailed off.

" I would be very disappointed — " Deacon Hale began, and then his voice trailed off too. Enoch had wheeled the horses and had called Nathan to ride to the barn and help him unload.

Nathan was glad to escape. He didn't know what he wanted to do. Teach? If he were sure he could teach with vision, teach in such a way that he could fire boys with an understanding of great men and inspire them to great deeds! He didn't know. But he was becoming more and more certain that the ministry was not the call he would answer.

" There's to be singing school tonight, John tells me," Enoch said as they rode toward the barn, high on the bouncing load.

As he packed the hay into the mow, Nathan thought

how pleasant it would be to sit by Alice in the wagon tonight on the way to the sing. There were so many things he wanted to tell her, and there had been so little opportunity. He wanted to tell her of what he had learned about the stars: how that group they had always thought looked like an armored knight with belted sword must also have looked so to the ancients, for they had made up stories about him and called him Orion. He wanted to tell her about the poems Tallmadge wrote. Some of them he could recite to her. And he wanted her to know about Hull, the sophomore whom he hoped to be more intimate with next year as an upperclassman. He might even tell her how Hull had befriended him the night he smoked his first pipe, but he wasn't sure about that.

At dinner, over great slabs of hot corn bread swimming in maple sirup, bean soup with chunks of fresh pork floating in it, and thick apple pie, plans were made for the evening. They would do the chores early so that they could get started to singing school by seven o'clock, as Enoch and Nathan were anxious to visit with friends whom they had not seen for a year.

"We'll drive Old Nell and Babe to the wagon," the Deacon said. "Enoch has asked for the rig and Queen."

Nathan looked at Enoch with interest. So his brother was going to beau one of the neighborhood girls!

"Who, Enoch?" he asked, his eyes teasing.

Enoch looked at his plate, and Alice blushed scarlet.

"Enoch has asked Alice to ride with him," Abigail said.

Nathan's spoon fell to the floor, and Joanna asked innocently, " Oh, can't I ride in the rig with Alice and Enoch? "

" Not this time, dear," Abigail answered. " Nathan wants you to ride with him so he can tell you stories about college."

Nathan, his spoon recovered, began eating. What right had Enoch to monopolize Alice? Wasn't she as much his sister as Enoch's? He was bitterly disappointed, for he had planned so happily all the things he was going to tell her as they rode over the moonlit hills.

Suddenly the realization struck Nathan that it was not as his sister that Enoch was taking Alice, but as his girl. The idea confounded him. He had never thought of Alice as having beaux, and yet she was growing up. But for it to be Enoch, who was practically her brother — He had lost interest in singing school and was surprised at his own change of spirits. Was it because Alice was not to ride in the same wagon with him? Could it be that he too was thinking of her in some other light than as a sister? Puzzled, he pushed back his chair and rose from the table, thinking to go out in the orchard, alone with his thoughts, or down to the old secret nook in the pasture. What was it Alice had written? That she had not been there since he left?

" Excuse yourself, son," the Deacon commanded. " Have they taught you to forget manners at college? "

Embarrassed, Nathan stammered an excuse and bolted out the door. He did not see Alice's troubled eyes follow him.

So he was surprised when bareheaded, bare-armed,

and breathless, she let herself down over the bank to the grassy carpet where he sat.

" Back to our secret nook," she said. " It's the first time I've been here since we said good-by." Breathlessness gave her words a quick rush. " Nathan."

" Yes? "

" About my going with Enoch — " She would not look at him, and the slow color was washing her throat. " I didn't know what to do. Ma said since he asked me I should accept as all the other girls would be going with escorts."

" Oh." Nathan's voice was flat.

" I told her I didn't see why I couldn't go with both of you as my escorts, but she said Enoch had already asked your pa for the rig so she guessed I'd better go with him — " She broke off unhappily.

But Nathan suddenly smiled and spoke eagerly: " Maybe you and I can have the rig to go to the party Asher's having before we go back to school. I'll ask pa."

" O Nathan! " was all she said, but her tone brought back to him the little girl who used to think that everything he did was wonderful.

Too soon the vacation days ended and it was time to start back to New Haven for another year. Again there was the excitement of setting out, but the uncertainty of going into the unknown was no longer a part of it. Nathan knew now what lay ahead. He and Enoch would be upperclassmen this year, on an equal footing with Hull and the others. It would be good to get back. But the easy, companionable feeling of an old shoe for its mate, which had always existed between him and his older brother, had vanished. He had asked for the rig for Asher's party, and his father had allowed him to have it, perhaps seeing no reason to favor one boy over the other. Enoch had not seemed pleased.

Nathan found that leaving Alice behind was harder than it had been the fall before. But the fact that he and Enoch were departing together made the situation somewhat more endurable. At least *he* won't be here to take her out while I'm away, he thought.

Finally the good-bys were over, and the boys were on their way — back to a man's world where these strange emotions aroused by girls would have no part. Or so Nathan thought.

CHAPTER 6

Swift Seasons

WHEN THE class of '73 descended upon Yale as sophomores, it seemed to Nathan that Old Father Time picked up his skirts, laid down his scythe, and drank deep of the Fountain of Youth. For how else could the Old Man suddenly have developed a speed that raced the year away?

That winter he and Enoch were made members of the coveted Linonia. He took full advantage of its opportunities for debate and discussion.

"A man should never waste a moment," he declared emphatically one night to his brother Linonians. "Life's short enough at best, and a fellow has to use every minute, with so many things to be done in the world."

"Then you're just the man for our next program," spoke up young Timothy Dwight, who, though a tutor, was not much older than the boys themselves and was destined years later to be president of Yale. "You can lead the next discussion."

Dwight was popular among the boys and a good friend of Nathan's. His suggestion met with approval.

"Up with Hale Secundus!"

Nathan knew that as a rule the discussions were led by juniors and seniors, or by tutors, and that his fellow members were showing unusual faith in his ability by nominating him, a sophomore, for next week's leader.

" If you think I can do it — " he began uncertainly.

" Of course you can! "

" Why not? "

" You're our man."

He spoke hesitantly: " What's the topic for next meeting? If it's something I can handle — "

The secretary turned the pages of his book and read, " ' January 26 — Topic: " What Thing in the World Is Most Delightful to Man?" ' "

Nathan's eyes lighted. Here was a question well worth discussing. He flashed Timothy Dwight a smile. What great fun it would be to lead a discussion on such a subject!

Often, in the week before the Linonia meeting, Nathan's mind was concerned with the problem they were to discuss. His own convictions were formed, but he found himself wondering what the great of the past would have thought. To Julius Caesar, wouldn't conquest have been the great delight? To Aristotle, philosophy? To Roger Williams, social reform?

He discussed the subject avidly with Tallmadge, whose ideas differed sharply from his. He was deep in argument with this friend as they hurried to astronomy class one morning.

" But you're arguing for something that just isn't important," Nathan was insisting. " It's what we *are* that matters, and that's not measured by what we have but by what we do."

" Oh-ho, Damon and Pythias in a quarrel," a jovial voice exclaimed. John Palsgrave Wyllys blocked their path. " You know ou can't do that. We'd hate to lose our Damon and ythias."

" No danger," Tallmadge grinned.

" There are lots of things we don't agree on," Nathan said, " but we're friends." It had been inevitable that he and Tallmadge should become known on the campus as Damon and Pythias. He had other warm friends: Roger Alden, James Hillhouse, who was one day to be treasurer of Yale, and Marvin, a future doctor, but it was to Tallmadge — Tallmadge who in the Revolution would manage General Washington's secret service — that he gave his closest allegiance.

The night of the Linonia meeting, Nathan and Tallmadge came together to the bare classroom where the society met. Nathan took the rostrum, as was the custom for the leader, while Tallmadge sat by Enoch in the assemblage below. Some of the members were slow in arriving, and the others amused themselves while they waited by poking good-natured fun at Nathan and his " pulpit."

" All you need's the long-tailed coat," Alden called to him.

" Brother Hale! " Hillhouse rose to address him with an exaggerated show of respect.

Nathan turned a little pink under the raillery.

Wyllys disagreed, however, with this characterization of Hale Secundus.

" This man's too eloquent to wear the cloth," he said

with a pretense of deep seriousness. " He could outtalk the devil, and then there'd be nothing left to preach about."

The last member straggled in, and the serious business of the meeting began. The Linonians always took their discussions seriously.

" Brother Linonians," Nathan began, " the topic for discussion this evening is, ' What Thing in the World Is Most Delightful to Man? ' Let us first examine the meaning of the word ' delightful.' The dictionary defines it as ' that which brings extreme satisfaction, joy, or great pleasure — a high degree of gratification of mind or sense.' Thus we see that delightful means much more than pleasurable; that it refers to something deeper, more worth-while, more lasting, which gives true soul satisfaction. I believe the most satisfactory thing in the world to man is performing brave and virtuous deeds."

Immediately a discordant chorus of approval and dissent broke out.

" Yes! "

" No! "

" He's right! "

" Not if by man you mean the *genus homo*."

Nathan rapped for order and continued: " Only through doing virtuous acts can a man get any real and lasting satisfaction. At the close of life, no man would say that the momentary pleasures of the senses had given him the greatest satisfaction in life, but that brave deeds done in a noble cause had brought him the truest delight. I am speaking of mankind in general.

Some men, lacking the insight to see truly and to evaluate correctly, may never experience the delight of noble action. But man in general, the *genus homo,* having in him the spark of God, will find brave and virtuous deeds the most satisfying."

Applause resounded through the room as Nathan sat down.

" Mr. Chairman! "

Tallmadge was on his feet. Nathan gave him a grin.

" Brother Tallmadge."

" Brother Linonians," Tallmadge said earnestly, " I disagree with the stand taken by our chairman. It seems obvious to me that he is talking about only a select few. Our question is, ' What will bring the greatest delight to *man?* ' — which means to the majority of men, not to a select few. The answer, I am sure, is wealth."

Loud acclamations of agreement greeted the declaration.

" Mr. Chairman! "

" Mr. Chairman! "

Now that two views had been presented, everyone wanted to talk at once.

" Order! Order! " Nathan commanded. " Mr. Hillhouse. The Chair recognizes Mr. Hillhouse."

Long of leg, dark of skin, and high of cheekbone, James Hillhouse stood before the meeting. " It all depends on the kind of man, doesn't it? " he drawled. Hillhouse never got excited, never was in a hurry. " Hale's right on the kind of man he's talking about; Tallmadge, on the kind he's speaking of. Now, which of the two kinds predominates? "

Hillhouse sat down, perfectly willing to let the others decide the issue he had raised.

" But every man has a spark of the divine in him," Nathan answered instantly. " That makes them all my kind of man."

" Maybe so, but they still want money," Alden pointed out.

The argument had only begun. Far into the night they debated. Dwight and Hull and Robinson and Enoch lined up with Nathan, but the opposition was strong, at least in numbers. Nathan still disapproved when, at midnight, a motion was carried to write into the minutes that the majority of the Linonians had come to the conclusion that " virtuous men will take the greatest delight in virtuous actions, but what is most delightful to most men is the acquisition of wealth." He didn't believe it was true.

" It's because you're one of those ' virtuous men ' that you can't see it our way, Nathan," Tallmadge said to him as the meeting broke up. " You make the mistake of believing that what's true for you is true for all men."

The day following the Linonia meeting brought a break in routine for the Hale brothers and a question more important to them at the moment than the one debated the night before. Nathan was bounding down the steps of Connecticut Hall, intent on getting out to a game of soccer, when something caught his eye and stopped him abruptly.

" Whoever — " he began in surprise, and the next moment was running out toward the hitching rack. For there stood a familiar gray horse.

" Good Old Nell! " he shouted as he ran. The horse whinnied softly at his approach.

" Who rode you down? " he said, stroking her nose. " How is everybody? Did you bring the Deacon? " The horse nuzzled him fondly. " Who's your friend? " he went on, looking over at the bay tied to the other post. " Oh, Reverend Fry's horse. Did pa ride down with the Reverend? " He gave the horse another pat. " I'll be back later. Maybe I can find a lump of sugar."

Nathan hurried to Enoch's room. As he approached, he heard the Reverend Fry's nasal tones and Enoch's quiet voice, but not the Deacon's deep, throaty resonance. A chill of foreboding clutched him. Was something wrong at home? Were he and Enoch needed, and had the Deacon sent the horse for them?

The moment he entered the room, Reverend Fry caught the question in his eyes. " I was coming this way, Nathan, so your father asked me to bring a horse down for one of you to ride home. He wants you boys measured for new clothes."

Nathan knew a vast relief. " Which one of us? " he asked.

" Whichever is best able to get away," the minister replied. " Your father said he would leave that to your judgment."

" Enoch," Nathan said with a grin, " if they measure you for both our suits, I'll burst the seams of mine and dangle out the sleeves; and if they measure me, you'll rattle in yours like a scarecrow."

Enoch gave a wry smile. Nathan had outgrown him

the past two years in both height and breadth.

"The Deacon didn't think you should both leave your studies," Reverend Fry said.

"I've got that examination coming up in advanced trig," Enoch worried.

Nathan said, "I can go or I can stay, whichever you prefer."

"You'd better go tomorrow morning," Enoch decided reluctantly.

The world was clad in white when Nathan set out in the gray, cloudy March dawn to cover the sixty miles of narrow, twisting road to Coventry. Though a promise of spring was in the air, a dreary winter landscape stretched out on either side of him, hour upon hour. The little round haycocks in the fields, topped with a coating of smooth, hard snow, reminded him of the cupcakes Abigail and the girls baked in the big kitchen at home and then covered with shiny white frosting. Bordering the fields, the gray stone walls humped over the hills like huge gray caterpillars.

Suddenly, as he rode over the crest of a hill, he caught sight of a little unpainted, deserted house in the valley below, held in a clump of trees like a deserted bird's nest. Houses were so human, he thought. This one now — its story must have ended sadly even though it had probably begun with someone's high hopes and dreams. It must have known love and toil, happiness and hardship, and, finally, hopelessness and defeat. What would it be like to know unhappiness and defeat, he wondered.

Early dusk found him still on the road, but passing fields that were now familiar. The sky in the west was a soft, muted purple. Something about Neighbor Forbes's hillside where the timber used to stand looked strange to him in the fading light. It seemed to be covered with a colony of small, crouching black-and-white animals. He laughed as he drew closer and saw that his animals were snow-caked stumps Old Man Forbes had not yet grubbed out.

One more hill, then the lane, and he would be home again. It was only six months this time since he had left it. Would Alice be glad to see him? Was she watching the lane, wondering whom the gray horse was carrying toward Coventry? He was sure she preferred him to Enoch, but he was sorry if her preference made Enoch unhappy, for he was fond of his brother. He wished Enoch would become interested in some other girl.

The family were at supper when he arrived. Should he knock, pretending to be a caller, or should he throw open the door and surprise them? His own eagerness decided him. He burst in with a whoop like one of David's Indian war cries, and no tribe of Indians could have made more noise than the tribe of Hales as they jumped up from the table, scrambling over their benches, to greet him.

" Careful! You'll tip the table," Abigail laughed.

The family swarmed around him. How he loved them all!

" You're getting to be a man, Nathan, and we're so proud of you," Abigail said. He had filled out his height in the last six months and was broad-shouldered and narrow-hipped. His forehead was high and full, his features regular and fine. With his light-brown hair and blue, sparkling eyes, he was good to look at.

Elizabeth put on another plate. She walked straight as a young sapling in her gray calico dress as she went to the cupboard for the extra dishes.

" We didn't expect you today," the Deacon said. " I didn't figure you'd be able to get away so soon."

Nathan explained about Enoch's examination. His own situation had been such that President Daggett said he could leave at once, but he was to return within the week. He sought Alice's eyes as he talked, and found that a cloud obscured them. Had he been a fool, he wondered, to think she favored him?

Scarcely were they through supper when there was a knock at the door.

" Would that be Asher already? " Nathan asked.

" I think it's Elijah Ripley," Elizabeth answered. Nathan looked at his sister. Was Ripley courting her? Well, he could do worse. She looked sweet and serious. As for Ripley, he would be a fine catch. He was probably the most well-to-do young merchant in Coventry and came from an excellent family. Although Elijah had not gone to college, he seemed to be well-read and to have a good mind.

Nathan was glad to see him. The visitor was much older than he — probably thirty — but interested in the same things he was.

" What about the Sons of Liberty down at Yale, Nathan? " Elijah asked.

" We're thriving," Nathan answered.

" Then you're a member? " the Deacon asked quickly.

"Yes. So's Enoch, and Hull, and Tallmadge, and Dwight — all the fellows with any spirit. Of course, a few oppose it, still standing firm in the belief that whatever our mother country does must be right."

"But it isn't!" argued Ripley. "Being taxed without being represented in government is never right. And this having to send our products to England to be marketed by an agent who sends us back no money, but such goods as he chooses — I tell you, the Colonies aren't going to endure it forever."

"That's what we in Sons of Liberty think," Nathan agreed. "They've no right to treat us so unjustly. Our forefathers came to this country for liberty and went through many hardships to attain it. Now it's being taken away from us."

"But perhaps it does not rest with us to take such matters into our hands," the Deacon put in. "There is a Power greater than all our human power that guides our destinies. The God of righteousness will take care of us if we are patient."

"It's hard to be patient," Nathan objected. "Perhaps He means that we must do something about it."

Talk turned to other things. Nathan, going with John to put his horse in the barn, returned to find the Deacon reading, the smaller children playing on the floor, Abigail sewing, and the girls knitting. And Elijah Ripley was sitting, not beside Elizabeth, but beside Alice.

So that was the way the wind was blowing! Nathan didn't like it. Yet Ripley was so much older and more sedate than Alice that surely she would not be interested. After all, the fact that Ripley chose to sit beside her didn't mean that she was showing him favor. He saw that Alice was embarrassed and he thought Ripley should see it too and should absent himself accordingly. But Ripley sat on, making pleasant conversation, until the Deacon began to yawn and look meaningfully at his big gold watch.

Nathan went back to school at the end of the week with a question in his mind. Abigail had spoken of Ripley often and with obvious approval. He had wanted to speak to Alice about the matter before he left, but it seemed hardly the thing to do. After all, what could he say? That he had hoped she would sit at home and wait for him to finish college? That would sound selfish. All he could do was to hope that Alice would not be attracted by this older suitor. But a little undercurrent of worry tugged at his mind as he traveled the slow miles back to New Haven. And because he seemed unable to shake the worry after he was back at school, he mentioned it to Enoch, as casually as possible.

" By the way," he said, when he had given Enoch the news from home and the messages which the family had sent him, " Alice seems to have a beau."

Enoch started noticeably. " What! "

This makes three of us, Nathan thought. Aloud he said, " Yes, Elijah Ripley."

Enoch was incredulous. " He's twice her age! "

" I know," Nathan agreed, and then voiced his own fears. " But he's well off and not half-bad-looking, to say nothing of being a very nice fellow."

" Yes, but — "

" Well, after all, she's young and pretty and full of life. She can't sit home all the time and knit." Nathan was using the argument he had used on himself.

" She could for a while," Enoch answered from the depths of his own concern. Then he tried to twist the meaning. " That is, she's pretty young to be going about much, isn't she? "

" Oh, I don't know. John was born when ma was only sixteen," Nathan pointed out.

Other interests, however, crowded Alice to the back of his mind. He had gone out for crew, and as spring came on, he practiced almost daily with Gridley, trying to improve his stroke.

One gray afternoon, when he met his roommate at the bay for their usual workout, Gridley greeted him with, " That's a sort of bad-looking cloud, don't you think? "

Nathan cocked an eyebrow at his roommate. " Trying to get out of this? "

" No, but I think that cloud looks as if it means business."

Nathan glanced up at a black mass rolling like a huge ball of yarn across the western sky. He whistled.

" Maybe you're right, but it won't get here for a while. Let's do what we can before it hits. We won't go out far."

" We'd better *not* go out far," Gridley agreed uneasily.

Soon the boat was gliding as smoothly as a sled over

hard-packed snow. Intent on the work, Nathan did not again notice the rapidly gathering storm until a raindrop splashed on his hand.

At the same moment Gridley shouted: " Hey! We've got to turn back."

The cloud had become a huge, dark-gray blanket, spreading itself across nearly the whole vault of the sky. A sudden gust of wind struck at the boat, almost wrenching the oar from Nathan's grasp.

" Turn her! " Gridley shouted. " Head for shore! "

Pitting all their strength against the mighty force of the wind, they managed finally to head the boat toward land. Then the wind tore control from them and spun them around. Gloom had thickened to blackness and the vivid flashes of lightning, running down the sky like molten silver, showed Gridley's tense face.

" Hold her till it dies down," Nathan cried through a rift in the wind.

" We'll capsize! " came Gridley's voice.

Nathan caught the fear in it. But they couldn't be far from shore, he felt sure, and they both *could* swim. A vicious wave slapped the boat roughly, making it career madly.

" We're gone! " Gridley cried.

But the boat righted itself. Then, suddenly, the wind seemed to lose its fury as though tired of wasting so much energy in wrath.

" Now we can turn her," Nathan called.

Together they pulled, working the boat steadily in the direction from which they had come.

" There we are," Nathan cried, catching sight of the

beach as a sudden flash of lightning revealed a white wedge like a gash in a log.

" Thank the Lord," Gridley said fervently. " I never thought we'd see this shore again, and that's the Gospel truth."

Nathan threw back his head and laughed. " And *I* never thought that we *shouldn't*. And *that's* the Gospel truth," he replied.

CHAPTER **7**

Disquieting Moments

TIME IN Nathan's junior year raced past important distance markers with coattails flapping. One marker represented the production of Linonia's play *The Toy Shop*. Another was his election as Chancellor of Linonia, the highest office of the campus' most respected organization. Still a third marked the day he broke the Yale broad-jump record and was carried high on the shoulders of brother Linonians through the streets of New Haven to the chant of:

> " Hale Secundus, Hale Secundus,
>   Good old Brother Hale,
>   Jumped the jump that made us famous,
>   Brought renown to Yale."

Then came the week the Deacon rode down to New Haven on a visit, with word that Alice was surely going to " land " Elijah Ripley. Time left a deep impression as it passed that marker, and Nathan gazed after it aghast. For time seemed to be carrying Alice on a swift tide away from him.

When he and Enoch went home for their last vacation — they would be seniors when they returned to school — he found a household strangely altered. Elizabeth was gone, married to Samuel Rose, who would soon take over his aging father's medical practice. John too had married — Alice's older sister, Sally — and was living with his young wife in his father's home. But she could not, it seemed to Nathan, fill Elizabeth's place.

However, there were things that remained unchanged — the Deacon's autocratic rule and Abigail's steady love. Nathan realized more and more how much his stepmother meant to them all.

" You know," he said to her, coming to stand beside her as she thumped the dasher in the big barrel churn, " whatever I do in the world that's worth doing at all — if I do anything — will be done because of you."

" Why, Nathan," Abigail said in surprise, " you can't mean that! "

" I mean every word of it. I'll never forget the first day you came. After you'd gone upstairs, I stood here in the kitchen and thought what a difference you would make in our lives, and how beautiful you were."

" You thought me beautiful? "

" I still do." He smiled at her. " And — " he had often wanted to say this to her, but until growing up had made him less self-conscious, he had never been able to — " I loved you from the minute you came."

Tears were in her eyes. " I'll never forget what you've said, Nathan. Especially will I remember when you do those great things."

He laughed softly. " But I'm only going to teach."

" You'll do them," she said. There was a singing conviction in her voice.

But the next night when Elijah Ripley came to call on Alice, all Nathan's joy at being home and the glowing warmth born of Abigail's faith in him vanished. He sat by the fire, whittling on a hickory whistle, and did not realize that Abigail was studying him, seeing that he was not joining in the conversation.

Nor did he know that by the set of his lips and the way he held his head, she suddenly came to realize that he was in love with Alice. Had he been studying his stepmother, he might have seen her consternation at what she had done by bringing Alice into a home where there were boys her own age. And he might have seen compassion for himself, born of his stepmother's realization that Alice would certainly marry Elijah Ripley because the Deacon had determined that it should be so. And finally, he might have seen that, for the first time, Abigail felt old, weighted down by living with a man so impregnable as the Deacon.

But Nathan was not studying Abigail, as she had been studying him. He was watching no one, in fact, until Enoch, his shoulders slumped, suddenly got up and went out. Then Nathan raised his head.

Enoch's given up, he thought, but I haven't.

With every downward stroke of his knife, he was planning a course of action. Alice wasn't married to Ripley, or engaged to him, as far as he knew. He wasn't sure that she wanted to be. Certainly she was not the **carefree**, vivacious girl who used to laugh and chatter and dance about like a wood sprite. Either being with Ripley had changed her or she was unhappy. He must get her alone and learn the truth. They were no longer children, too young to know their own minds. If she didn't love Ripley and did love *him* — He remembered the way she had come to him in their secret nook to tell him she didn't want to go with Enoch to singing school. But that was two years ago. She had always shared her thoughts with him, and done little special things for him and, he thought, had a special smile for him. But perhaps she was just fond of him as a brother. Well, he had to find out — that, and whether or not she loved Ripley.

The evening was a long one, but finally Ripley left, after sedately shaking hands all around, beginning with Abigail and the Deacon and ending with Alice. John and his wife and the younger children went up the narrow stairs to their cold, high-ceilinged bedrooms as the Deacon locked the doors and fixed the fire. Alice and Abigail kneaded down the big pans of bread dough, which had stood rising since supper. Nathan and Enoch stood silently by the mantel, Enoch staring into the bright patterns of the fire and Nathan gazing at the coat of arms above it.

Enoch said in his quiet way: " Well, guess I'll be off to bed. Coming, Nathan? "

" Soon," Nathan replied, but made no move to follow Enoch to the stairs. Alice and Abigail were washing the dough from their hands, and the Deacon was still winding his watch. The sound seemed very loud in the quiet room.

Nathan cleared his throat as Alice started toward the stairway. " Alice " — he had hoped his father would go up before Alice and Abigail, but since he hadn't — " I'd like to speak to you a moment before you go upstairs." His voice sounded hollow and strange.

The Deacon looked up from under his bushy black brows. " It is late, son, and time Alice was in bed."

" I'm sorry, father, but I won't keep her long." Nathan spoke with some of the Deacon's own determination.

A flush ran into Alice's cheeks.

" You will have plenty of time to talk tomorrow," the Deacon said in a tone that was meant to close the subject.

Alice, still fearful of her stepfather, started toward the stairs.

" What I have to say must be said tonight," Nathan insisted firmly.

The Deacon looked at his son in surprise. He was not used to having his authority questioned. " Young man, you will — " He got no farther. Abigail, who had never before questioned his absolute authority, had laid her hand on his arm.

" Let him have his way this once," she said gently. " Come, let us go up to bed."

The Deacon, surprised at her interference, followed her, without a word, to the foot of the stairs. There he turned back to say sternly to Nathan, " Your conduct is unbecoming to one of your years and training."

" I'm sorry, father," Nathan replied respectfully.

" See that you make your conversation brief," the

Deacon added curtly. " I shall be waiting to hear you come up the stairs."

Nathan closed the stair door and turned back to find Alice before the fireplace, her hands clasped tightly and her face drained of color.

" Nathan," she said in a troubled voice, " you shouldn't have defied your father."

" I had to, Alice. I had to talk to you now or I couldn't have slept all night. Alice, I have to know if you love Ripley."

She did not answer, so he went on, " If you've told him you're going to marry him — "

Alice's voice broke in. " I haven't told him I'm going to marry him. He hasn't asked me! " All at once the old twinkle was in her eyes.

" But when he does? "

" You think he will? "

" Alice, don't tease. I've got to know."

The twinkle was gone from her eyes. " No, Nathan, I don't think I love him. He's been ever so nice to me, and I've been happy going places with him, but — " She paused in confusion at the sudden look of joy in his eyes.

He caught her hands. " I've been so afraid all these last months at college. Every message that came from home — I was terrified for fear it would say you were married. There's one other question." She looked so sweet to him, standing there in her long blue calico dress with its high neck and tight, long sleeves, and its full skirt gathered in at the waist. " Alice, do you — do you happen to love *me?* "

The night was very still. Only the ticking of the old clock on the mantel broke the quiet, and the beating of his heart sounded loud in Nathan's ears as he waited for her answer.

She no more than whispered the words. " I guess I've always loved you, Nathan."

.   .   .   .

The next morning as Abigail watched Alice skip about the kitchen on winged feet, she was sure how things had gone the night before between Nathan and her daughter. What she did not see was how it was going to work out, how it was going to end. Nathan still lacked a year of graduation; and after that, unless he were lucky enough to get a tutorship, he would have to teach a couple of years before he could support a wife. She saw clearly the opposition that would come from the Deacon. Nathan would not be of age for three years, and for those three years the Deacon's word would be law. A heaviness pressed down upon her when she saw the look that passed between Alice and Nathan as they sat down to breakfast.

When the meal was over, and Nathan followed his father outside, she felt sure that it was to tell him of what had happened last night. And she knew, instinctively, that Alice was only waiting until they were alone to confide in her. How, she wondered, would this day end?

The kitchen cleared at last.

" Ma," Alice said, swishing a big bar of soft white lye soap about in the dishpan, " I want to tell you something — something so wonderful — " Her voice was a song.

" O God," Abigail prayed silently, " let her keep her joy! "

" It's about Nathan and me," Alice went on, the suds piling up and up in her pan as the color mounted in her cheeks. " Ma, you know what I'm trying to tell you? " Then it came in a rush. " Nathan loves me, and I love him, and we're going to be engaged until he's through school. Then maybe he can get a tutorship at Yale like Timothy Dwight. If he can't, he'll teach a year, and I'll be quilting and making my linen and — and then we'll be married. O ma, isn't it wonderful? " She clasped her hands together, and the little soap bubbles flew, catching the blue of her dress like tiny round mirrors.

" The soap," Abigail said helplessly.

" But aren't you glad, ma? " Alice asked, suddenly realizing that her mother had shown none of the delight she had expected from her.

Abigail took a long breath. " What about Elijah Ripley? " she asked.

" I don't love him, ma."

" I think he loves you, and unless I'm very much mistaken, he expects to marry you."

Alice was sobered. " I'll be sorry," she said sincerely, " if he's disappointed, but I've never said I'd marry him. It's Nathan I love."

Then Abigail struck the blow she dreaded to strike. " I'm afraid father won't approve," she said.

Alice stood motionless, her hands suddenly gone

limp in the dishpan. Then she asked in a very small voice from which all the joy had disappeared, " Why do you say that? "

" Because I know he's planning on your marrying Ripley."

At that, Alice suddenly came to life. " Nathan won't let him make me," she cried, her lips trembling. " He won't let him, because he loves me, and *he's* going to marry me. He won't let father make me marry somebody else."

Abigail found breathing difficult.

" Nathan's going to talk to father this morning," Alice went on. " He's going to tell him our plans, and ask him for my hand. He's going to explain it all to him — how all we want now is to be engaged."

The kitchen door was flung violently open. The Deacon charged angrily into the room. Nathan, with a set, white face, was close on his heels.

" What's all this nonsense? " the Deacon burst out, striding across the room to where Alice stood with dishwater dripping from her hands. " You're marrying Elijah Ripley, young woman, and I want no foolishness between you and Nathan."

Alice trembled under the Deacon's attack. She had always been afraid of bringing his wrath down upon her, and now it had come. Nathan, seeing her fright, came to her side and reached for her hand. Furious at what seemed insolent disregard of his command, the Deacon reached out swiftly and struck his son across the wrist.

" Father! " Nathan's arm fell to his side.

" You will disobey me, will you? " the Deacon roared.

Abigail stood by the table piled with dishes waiting to be washed. The floor seemed to be pulling at her feet as if it were quicksand. The weight of it crept up and up, through her limbs, to her heart. She couldn't even pray.

" I didn't mean to disobey you, father," Nathan said quietly. " But you can't force Alice to marry Elijah Ripley. If you won't allow us to be engaged, we'll wait for each other. You can't prevent our doing that. When I'm of age — "

The Deacon's face was purple. " When you're of age? When you're of age Alice will be settled in her own home and the mother of a family! "

A protest escaped Alice's lips.

" Go to your room! " the Deacon commanded her.

Just then the outside door opened and Enoch, coming in with a bucketful of water, stood in the doorway. So Nathan, his eyes said with understanding, had dared to defy his father.

The Deacon stamped out as Enoch set the bucket of water on the table.

Nathan, suddenly trembling, went out the door and took the opposite direction from the one his father had taken. But, before he had gone far, he came back and tossed a pebble against the window of Alice's room. When he saw her at the window, he motioned toward the pasture, then turned toward the secret nook.

She came through the hazel bushes so quietly that he did not know she was there until she spoke.

" Nathan," she called, her voice low.

In one bound he was across the little enclosure, which now seemed so much smaller than it had when they were children.

" It'll be all right," he said. " Don't cry! " He could have cried himself. He thought suddenly of the little deserted gray house he had seen when he rode home to be measured for new clothes. He had wondered then what unhappiness and grief were like. Now he knew. Only this was not going to end in defeat as the story of the little house seemed to have ended. He wouldn't let it! Let difficulties come; he would master them. He would *not* know defeat. He knew that probably some of the natural egotism of youth was mixed inextricably with his faith, but whatever it was, it gave him courage.

" Pa hasn't taken everything from us," he said. " He can't; he can only try. He can't make me stop loving you, or you stop loving me. It's too bad we can't be engaged as we'd planned, but we can wait. We can go on loving each other in our hearts, and time will go by before we know it."

" But it's so long, Nathan, till you're of age. I'll be twenty-one then too." Twenty-one seemed very old to her. By then, she feared, she might have lost her charms for him.

" Pa will relent long before that," he reassured her. " I'll work awfully hard, and maybe I can get a tutor-ship or a good school my first year out of college and we can be married then. That would only be a year."

Alice sighed. Nathan seemed so sure; perhaps he was right. But she couldn't help feeling a doubt.

" All we have to do is promise each other that we'll

wait." He stooped to pick a four-leaf clover and laid it in the palm of her right hand, pressing each leaf out firmly. " It'll bring us luck. Say after me, ' I, Alice, promise thee, Nathan — ' "

In an unsteady voice she repeated, " I, Alice, promise thee, Nathan — "

" That I will wait for thee — "

" That I will wait for thee — "

" Until such a time as we both can wed."

" Until such a time — " she stopped.

" Go on," he said, squeezing her fingers.

" Until such a time as we both can wed. Nathan," she added, troubled, " I think I ought to say, ' If I can.' "

Nathan's eyes were gentle. She was so terribly honest. " If you'd feel better about it — "

" If I can," she ended.

" Now make me say it," Nathan commanded.

" Say after me," Alice began, now smiling at him with darkly troubled eyes, " ' I, Nathan, promise thee, Alice — ' "

Solemnly he repeated the pledge.

" It sounds — something like a — a marriage cere-mony," she said when they had clasped hands over the four-leaf clover.

" It is — something like a marriage ceremony," Nathan agreed.

CHAPTER 8

First Defeat

THE FAMILY were gathered about the long plank table for supper the evening before Nathan was to return to Yale. The smell of fresh-baked rolls made them eager to begin the meal. But first they must sit through the Deacon's blessing.

" Dear God," he prayed, " we thank Thee for this our daily bread, and for the protection of our home. We thank Thee that Thou hast given us this country where we may be free to worship as we feel called upon to worship; we thank Thee for its fertile fields that yield up so bountiful a living; but, dear God, we pray that Thou mayest speedily bring about a cessation of the discord that exists between these colonies and the mother country. May the eyes of those that rule from the shores beyond the sea be opened, and may their hearts know understanding so that we may be extended a just and helping hand. And, dear God, for the hastening of Thy Kingdom we pray. May the Gospel of Jesus Christ, our Saviour, be brought speedily to all mankind. And for ourselves we ask that Thou wouldst forgive us our sins and lead us into the paths of righteousness. Dear God, bless our boys who are with us for these few days. Give them a safe journey on the morrow, and grant them the vision to see the glory of working for Thy name. May they allow no worldly thoughts or deeds to come into their lives to work to Thy dishonor. All of this we ask, dear God, in the name of Thy Son, Jesus Christ. Amen."

Scarcely able to contain herself until the Deacon finished, Joanna squirmed and twisted until Abigail laid a restraining hand on her arm. The instant the twelve bowed heads were raised, with a quick sigh of relief she asked politely but firmly for what she had so ravenously been craving.

" Dear God," she said, " please pass the rolls."

Without thought, Nathan threw back his head and roared. The little boys tittered, and Joanna, realizing what she had said, blushed scarlet.

" Children! " the Deacon roared, aghast at their sacrilege. " Joanna, leave the table this instant. Nathan! For anyone your age — You too leave the table! "

From the door, Nathan took a quick look back at the room. Alice gave him a frightened glance. He caught Enoch's eye, and all at once could read his brother's thoughts. Enoch knew what he had told Alice; Enoch knew of the scene in the kitchen. Enoch had resigned himself to losing Alice and thought that he, Nathan, was a fool to carry on a hopeless fight.

But it was *not* going to be a losing fight, Nathan thought grimly as he went toward the orchard.

As the autumn months sped by on red- and gold-winged feet, and winter, shod in white, crept over the

sleeping earth, Nathan planned that when spring came
he would somehow contrive to see Alice. Thoughts of
her filled his waking hours. Perhaps he would have to
go home to consult his father on the matter of a position
for the following year. He would find some excuse, for
he knew that when spring came he must go to her.

January and February, in that year of 1773, seemed
to drag endlessly, despite the gala celebration of Linonia's twentieth birthday, during which Nathan made
a speech, and despite a brief enforced vacation when
both he and Enoch, to say nothing of a dozen or so of
the other boys, came down with measles. He was so
anxious for spring to come that the late winter months
became a burden.

One day in late February, as he was crossing the
muddy college yard, holding up the folds of the long
black gown he wore as a senior, he caught sight of the
straight and unbending figure of the Reverend Fry on
his large bay horse. The minister had evidently been to
Connecticut Hall and was now on his way, for his
horse's head was turned toward town.

" Reverend Fry! " Nathan called after him.

The minister turned in his saddle, waved a greeting,
and halted his horse. Still holding his skirts high,
Nathan ran after him.

" I brought you and Enoch a letter," the Reverend
said as Nathan caught up with him. " I left it in Enoch's
room. I didn't have time to wait until one of you came
in. I'm on my way to Salem and I want to get as far as
possible tonight."

" Oh! " Nathan was disappointed. " I'd hoped you

could be persuaded to stay the night with us."

"Not this time. I'll stop and have a visit with you on my way back — about a month from now." The preacher's horse picked her feet out of the mud with a sucking sound as she moved off.

Nathan watched horse and rider until they disappeared, then turned his steps to the dormitory in which he had lived for three years and a half. He would hate to leave it, he thought, when commencement rolled around. He quickened his steps as he reached the entryway. A letter, Reverend Fry had said. Probably it would be from the Deacon, but there was the barest possibility that there might be one from Alice — tucked in somewhere if Abigail had sent them clothes. He bounded up the steps two at a time and down the corridor to Enoch's room, the tails of his black robe flying out like huge wings.

Enoch was at the window with the letter.

"Any clothes, cookies, or clanking coins?" Nathan asked, tossing his mortarboard on the bed and fumbling with the big hook at the throat of his gown.

"No, nothing but this letter," Enoch answered.

"From pa, of course?"

"Yes."

"Well, what's he say?" Nathan threw off his robe. Why hadn't Alice managed to slip Reverend Fry a pair of socks or a shirt so she could have tucked in a letter? It had been so long since he had seen her. He felt let down, depressed.

"He says they've had good snows, plenty of moisture to get the soil in good condition — "

Nathan scarcely listened. What did that matter? It was Alice he wanted to hear about, Alice he wanted to see. He didn't know if he'd wait till the end of March or the first of April to go home. Perhaps he could make arrangements to go now, soon.

" Nathan," Enoch said.

Nathan, standing close to him now, noticed for the first time that the letter shook in his brother's hand.

" What is it, Enoch? " he asked in alarm, putting out his hand.

Enoch did not give the letter to him. Instead, he wet his lips and said, " Nathan, Alice is married."

Nathan stared out into the rutted, muddy college yard — suddenly a dismal college yard — as Enoch laid the letter on the bed and slipped out of the room.

The spring! Nathan had counted so on the spring. But now he knew the spring would come too late.

He thought of the vows he and Alice had taken. " I, Alice, promise thee, Nathan — " For the first time, he saw a fateful significance in the way she had insisted, timidly yet surely, on adding to her vow, " If I can." He had passed it over lightly, indulgently, as another evidence of her meticulous honesty. Now he realized what it had meant — or did he? Could Alice have loved Ripley all the time and known she was going to marry him? But why, then, would she have said she loved *him?* That did not make sense — not for honest, clear-eyed, straightforward Alice, who could never tell less than the truth.

The words echoed pathetically in his ears: " If I can." She had added them, he decided, because she felt that she might not be strong enough to hold out against the Deacon. He felt sure it was his father who had overpowered her. Even had she been able to summon the courage to stand out against the Deacon, she would have thought it wrong, Nathan suspected, for she probably felt she owed his father respect and obedience for the home he had given her and the chance to be with her mother.

A fierce anger against the Deacon flamed in Nathan's heart. What right had he to interfere with other people's lives, to bend others with the force of his will because they were weaker than he? What right to twist them into unnatural, misshapen forms as the wind twisted the pines on the mountaintop till they were ugly and dwarfed and stunted? That was what he feared would happen to Alice.

If only he had been home, he thought in bitter regret, he would have defied his father. He would have taken Alice away and married her. Something. Anything. It would have been better if he had dropped everything, left college, and gone back to the farm. But he had thought he was doing the right thing to stay at school and strive to impress President Daggett with his ability to hold a tutorship the coming year. Now what did next year matter?

From the gayest of his group he became the bleakest. He knew that his friends were puzzled, but he could not talk to them about Alice, though they had known his plans and hopes. He had not even spoken of her to Enoch since the day his brother had given him the crushing news. And then one day he knew that Enoch must have said something of the truth to his friends, for all at once they were close to him again.

" What are you planning to do when graduation rolls around, Hale Secundus? " Timothy Dwight asked him one day. Nathan sensed an eagerness to arouse his interest.

" Take a trip to see my uncle in Portsmouth, I think," he replied, adding with a note of irony, " if I can get pa to spare one of his precious horses."

He was not going to Coventry when commencement was over. He couldn't bear the thought of the farm with Alice not there — Alice hurrying about the big kitchen setting the table or dishing up a steaming kettle of stew; Alice knitting by the fire in the evening; Alice laughing at the antics of the children; Alice running on happy feet to meet him in their secret nook. Nor did he think it wise to go home feeling as he did toward his father, for this would only widen the gap between them. He would not be able to control his anger, at least not yet. His chief regret at not going home was because of Abigail. He yearned for her sympathy and understanding. At first he wondered why she had failed to stop the Deacon's highhandedness. Why hadn't she stepped in as she had the night she took his father upstairs, to leave him alone with Alice? But evidently Abigail had been powerless in this greater struggle.

" But what about next year? " Timothy Dwight persisted, as Nathan committed himself no further than the trip he planned to take after commencement.

" Oh, I'll persuade them to give me a school somewhere."

"Not if you don't exhibit more enthusiasm than that."

"All right," Nathan agreed. "I'll try to get something lined up while I'm on this trip."

"Good," Dwight said with satisfaction. "That's better."

Two months before commencement, Nathan wrote to his father, asking if he might borrow one of his horses to ride to Portsmouth as soon as the exercises were over. He explained that he wished to look for a school and that he would like to visit his Uncle Samuel, whose long experience in a Latin school should make him the very man to give good, practical advice to one entering the teaching profession. The Deacon approved. He would be very glad, he wrote, to have his brother Samuel, whom he had not seen in twenty years, make the acquaintance of one of his sons. He would send two horses down at commencement, one for Enoch's trip home, the other for Nathan's journey.

Nathan was relieved. Now he could go through examinations and commencement with one thing off his mind — and he needed a clear mind for the grilling days ahead. Six months had eased the loss of Alice. With sufficient will power he could work over and above it, ignoring it during the day.

Finally, commencement came — the day toward which he and the other thirty-five seniors of the class of 1773 had been working for four years. Sometimes it seemed to him that he had been living on Brick Row forever; and again that it was only yesterday that he had straddled Old Nell and started down the lane from home on this great adventure.

Although commencement day found in the audience the parents of many of the thirty-six black-robed young men on the platform, Deacon Hale was not among them. He had written that he felt he could not leave John alone during haying.

The whole village of New Haven, Nathan thought as his glance ran over the audience, seemed to have turned out to the exercises. Here and there he saw a familiar face — a girl whom Tallmadge had been beauing around, and dark, handsome Benedict Arnold, whose apothecary shop he had frequented so much in the past four years. He had never exactly come to like the suave, self-sufficient young druggist, though he admired his clever mind. He couldn't put his finger on the reason for his dislike. Perhaps it was that he found Arnold a little too egotistical, a little too determined on worldly success.

Nathan continued to study the faces in the audience. There was nothing else in the world so interesting as people. Suddenly a young man near the back of the room turned his head. Nathan sat bolt upright. Could that be — It was. It was Hull. Good old Hull, who had finished the previous year, back to see the class of '73 graduate. Hull caught his eye and gave him a smile and a wave that were almost a shout.

Nathan felt more warmed than he had felt at any time since word of Alice's marriage had frozen his heart. He wished this business of the exercises were over so that he and Hull could take a stroll out to Gull Rock as they used to do. He didn't know when he had last taken that walk. The keen pleasure he had known in little things — the delicate coloring in a shell, the white wings of a gull, the throaty cry of the foghorn — had always been doubly sweet for the thought that someday he would share them with Alice. When this joy was taken away, he had closed his eyes to their beauty. But now that Hull was back — Hull, who had felt the same pull of beauty — Yes, with Hull, that very afternoon, he would walk along the shore and see again.

But the exercises had begun. Williams was giving an oration on "Prejudice." A dialogue followed on the three learned professions. That meant Nathan was coming up next, with Robinson, Samson, and Tallmadge, to debate whether woman should have a greater opportunity for education. They were being called up now. Robes flapping, they took their places.

Presently the exercises were over. Nathan had been cited for highest honors in the classics, and for more additional honors than any other member of the class. It should have been a day of triumph, but he felt no exultation. He had wanted all this for Alice — the diploma, that he might get a position worthy of her, and the honors, that he might get an immediate appointment. He was glad the Deacon had not come, for his presence would have made things more bitter. But if Abigail could have been there —

Ah, there was Hull, coming up to wring his hand in congratulation. He would take that walk with Hull and then, perhaps, feel better.

CHAPTER 9

Memorable Meeting

STARTING FOR Portsmouth
the following morning, Nathan did feel better, although the business of bidding the fellows good-by had
not been a joyous one. Now that the partings were over,
he knew again something of that excitement of anticipation that he had experienced when he first set out
for Yale.

This was the fourth of September. The ocean breeze
had an invigorating touch. He had chosen to take the
shore road by way of New London, the road Benjamin
Franklin's penny post followed. He was anxious to see
Boston, for he had heard a great deal about this city,
the city where some of the most influential citizens of
the Colonies lived, the city where a liberty pole had
been erected at the beginning of the Stamp Act agitation.

A stay overnight on the road would be a new experience. He hoped he could find an inviting tavern about
dusk. The gaily painted swinging signboards intrigued
him, and they bore the most romantic-sounding names:
The Pig and Whistle, The Jolly Roger, The Tiger's

Paw, The Bunch of Grapes.

However, as the lengthening shadows of late afternoon faded into early twilight, and mile after mile now brought no new signboard at the side of the road, Nathan began to feel uneasy, for he had heard many tales of highway robbery and murder. He did not want to lose the money the Deacon had generously sent down for his trip; nor, for that matter, would he want to lose his life. Just as he was beginning to wonder if he should have stopped at the last inn he had passed during the afternoon, he saw lights ahead and, as he drew nearer, the swinging sign for which he had been looking. He strained his eyes and made out, in the waning light, its name, " The Happy Warrior."

The inn itself lived up to the picturesqueness of its name. There was a short, red-faced, potbellied proprietor. There were crude, hand-hewn wooden tables and chairs about the room into which he stepped, and men in homespun, like his own, sitting about. A huge fire burned on the hearth, and over it a spit was being turned. The delicious odor of roasting pork filled the room. He suddenly realized that he was hungry.

He was shown upstairs to an unfinished gabled room, in which he left his belongings. He glanced briefly at the sparse furnishings and grimaced as the cornhusk mattress rattled warningly when he sat on it. He went back down the crude stairs to the room below, and, glancing about, noticed that all the tables except one were occupied. He made his way toward this table, noting as he went how ardently the men were talking together in little groups. He seated himself, ordered dinner, and turned his attention to the other occupants of the room.

Now and then he caught a word or a phrase from the group by the fire. " Liberty " seemed to be often repeated, and " injustice," and " independence." He began to eat rapidly, that he might finish his meal and join them, for he had strong views on the subject of the Colonies' relations with the mother country.

Suddenly he became aware of a change in the room. Looking about to discover its cause, he saw the burly innkeeper hastening toward the door, trailed by a queue of followers who peered over and around him as he threw open the door and called back over his shoulder: " 'Tis the coach, gentlemen. 'Tis the coach."

Nathan wondered what notable passengers the coach might set down, but was unwilling to leave his applesauce and pork to join those who had followed the innkeeper.

A few moments later the door opened again, and the bouncing little proprietor, with great ceremony, ushered in his guest. The stranger, tall, square-shouldered and erect, was dressed in the fashion of the well-to-do gentleman of the day — a tricorn hat over the curls of his white wig, and a colorful blue coat adorned with large gold buttons over his yellow satin waistcoat.

" This way, Colonel, this way," the innkeeper beamed, bobbing and bowing as he led his guest through the room and up the steep stairs.

So the stranger, Nathan thought, was a colonel. Certainly he looked the part. Those who had gone out to meet the coach were returning, and the room became fired with excitement. Nathan, listening eagerly to catch what was said, did not note the innkeeper's return. Suddenly, however, he heard the fellow's voice, purring with deference, at his very elbow.

" I will have a table for you in one moment, sir, if you'll just take a seat by the fire."

Nathan, looking up quickly, saw the stranger towering above him. He jumped up.

" Take this table, sir," he said.

But the tall stranger, bowing his thanks, stepped to the other side of the table and pulled out the chair opposite Nathan's.

" Finish your meal, young man," he said in a voice as stately as his bearing. " I shall be glad to share your board."

A hush had wiped out the noise of the room as completely as a wet rag wipes a child's slate. Nathan was aware of every eye being upon his table.

The gentleman across from him said, " My name is Washington."

Nathan tried to control the sudden excitement in his voice. " Not George Washington, of Virginia? " Washington! George Washington! Eating at his table, talking to him! " You were one of our favorite heroes at Yale, sir."

" So? Then you are a Yale man."

" Yes, sir; I am one of a class of thirty-six who were graduated yesterday. We often discussed your courage and sagacity in Braddock's campaign."

" You Yale men discuss the affairs of modern times then as well as of antiquity? " Washington asked.

" Oh, yes — in our literary societies, and in Benedict Arnold's apothecary shop, where everybody congregates downtown."

" Then you talk of the present distress of the Colonies in their relationship with the mother country? "

" More than we talk of anything else."

" And what are your views on the subject? "

The color was high in Nathan's cheeks. " That we cannot afford to submit to such treatment." But he was interested in hearing Washington's views, not in expressing his own. " Would it be presuming too much, sir, to ask your opinion, as a military man? "

Washington smiled. " I am hardly a military man, Mr. — Mr. — ? "

" Hale," Nathan supplied. " Nathan Hale."

" I can hardly speak as a military man at present, Mr. Hale, having known no active service for fifteen years. But as a businessman, I would say that the situation is deplorable, and that you are absolutely right in feeling that we cannot afford to submit to such treatment."

" But what's to be done about it, sir? "

" I am afraid, my young friend," the Colonel replied slowly, " that in the ultimate situation we shall find it necessary to resort to armed resistance."

Nathan felt his excitement rising. Before he could say that he held the same opinion, Washington was pushing his chair back from the table, his meal finished. He held out his hand. Nathan was on his feet in an instant.

" I am returning from a business trip to Boston and must go on by the early stage in the morning, Mr. Hale, so I shall retire to my room now. Thank you for letting me share your table."

Nathan bowed low. " Thank *you!* Thank you, sir, for the privilege."

Washington turned toward the stairs. He took one long step, then turned back and laid a hand on Nathan's shoulder.

" It's men like you that will lift the yoke of tyranny Britain is imposing on the Colonies," he said. Then he turned again toward the stairs and this time mounted them.

Nathan stood by the table watching the tall, erect figure. George Washington! George Washington had laid a hand on his shoulder and had given him a stirring challenge.

He reached Boston with the memory of George Washington still fresh in his mind. Here was the city of the massacre that had stirred the Colonies three years before. When news had reached New Haven that the British troops had fired on the people in the streets of Boston, killing three and mortally wounding two others, the college boys had flocked to the village square, where a rousing meeting had been held.

Nathan found an old gentleman who pointed out the very spot of the massacre and told of standing in the crowd and seeing the British fire. The Bostonian proudly showed him the liberty pole that had been erected in protest against the Stamp Act, and the great elm that had been hung with lanterns when the act was repealed. And he spoke of some of the town's leading citizens: of the two Adams cousins, Samuel and John, who were frank in their defiance of British authority, and of John Hancock, a prosperous merchant, who also spoke his mind.

Nathan loved the quaint streets of Boston, with their attractive, rich-looking shops, and the fine houses on Beacon Hill. He passed through Pudding Lane, and Corn Court, and Milk and Water Streets. He hated to leave this fascinating city. One window he could never pass without stopping. It was the window of a silversmith, and in it lay lovely hand-wrought chains, and ladies' brooches, and table silver, thin as a coin and as delicate as a flower. Finally he went in and purchased two silver spoons, one to take to his aunt and one to keep for Abigail. The silversmith's name was Paul Revere, and Nathan remembered it, for he thought a man who wrought such beauty must indeed revere beauty.

At Salem, he spent a whole afternoon watching the boats load and unload cargo at the wharves. He decided to spend the night in Salem, though he might have ridden much farther before dark had he not found the seaport so interesting. He had heard of Salem's witchcraft trials and had been horrified to think people had been ignorant enough to believe such superstitions and cruel enough to hang their friends and relatives. Here he was under the very shadow of Gallows Hill! The Linonians had discussed the horror at length, and had decided that the Colonies needed education to combat such atrocities. There was a rumor in the Hale household that, two generations before the Deacon's time, a minister in their family, who had preached strong sermons against the witches, later found his own wife accused of being one.

It was late afternoon of the next day when Nathan reached Portsmouth. His journey had borne fruit, for the experiences he had met and the places he had seen had put enthusiasm back into his voice and walk. As he rode down the street on which his uncle lived, he felt a tingle of excitement. These people he would meet were of his own flesh and blood and yet were strangers.

He found the house, a substantial, well-proportioned rectangular brick, with the usual large white pillars across the front and a white door set in a graceful brick arch. A graying man who resembled his father, but with less severity and more kindliness in his face, opened the door to him.

" My name's Hale, sir," Nathan said.

" Hale? " his uncle asked in surprise, raising a bushy eyebrow reminiscent of the Deacon's.

" Yes, sir. Nathan Hale, your brother Richard's boy."

A hand gripped his. " Richard's boy? Come in, come in. Mary! Mary! Come here, Mary."

Nathan instantly liked this hearty uncle and his wife Mary, a slight woman who looked quite elfin beside the six-foot-two of her husband. There were six children — three boys and three girls — the eldest a boy a little younger than Nathan. They were a happy family, just such a family as might have lived at Coventry, Nathan thought, if the iron hand of the Deacon had been lighter. Here he found a comradeship and a congeniality between the children and their parents that he and his brothers and sisters had never known. Not that his uncle was a lax disciplinarian, for he had been in the French and Indian War and was as much the major in his own home as he had been in the Army. But he was somehow a kindlier, more understanding, and less tyrannical man than his brother.

" You've another cousin living here," Uncle Samuel said that first evening at supper. " We'll have to have him over to meet you — the son of my brother next older than your father. He happens to be my namesake. He's reading law in Portsmouth, a brilliant young fellow. You'll enjoy meeting him."

Nathan did not have long to wait to make the acquaintance of young Sam Hale. The next day his uncle took him to see some of the interesting points of the city, and included a visit to the law office with which Sam was associated. Nathan found his cousin a charming young fellow, handsome, intelligent, and polished. He felt a little crude in his presence. Living in a city, attending fine parties, and knowing affluence had given Sam a polish he envied.

" Can you come over to supper with us tonight? " Uncle Samuel asked.

Sam pondered a second. " I'm sorry, Uncle Samuel, but I've accepted an invitation to the Rosemonts' for this evening. They're having a young crowd in to dance."

" Make it any other night. Tomorrow? "

" I'll be happy to come tomorrow night," Sam answered.

Nathan looked forward to the following evening. He

dressed carefully, not caring to have his cousin think a Yale man in any way the inferior of a Harvard man. Sam, like his uncle, had attended Harvard.

As Nathan was tying his big blue polka-dot tie, he heard the door open and close and his cousin Jane's bright voice as she ushered Sam in. He gave his hair a final touch with the brush and started downstairs. But at the foot of the steps he came to a sudden halt, embarrassed by what he saw in the front hall. Sam was kissing Jane, not lightly on the cheek, as Nathan might have thought permissible with one's cousin, but on the lips, long and hard. Nathan blushed as Sam drew away and looked up at him with a laugh, giving Jane a little pat as she started kitchenward.

" Lucky dogs we are, eh, Nathan, to have such pretty young wenches for cousins? Jane's the best for kissing, although Ellen's not far behind her. Give Ellen another year — "

Nathan was shocked. He had wondered if Sam were courting Jane or engaged to her. But at Sam's mention of kissing Ellen as well, there was only one interpretation: this flashing cousin took every opportunity to kiss a pretty girl, whether or not she happened to be a relative.

Sam, noticing his confusion, laughed. " What? Haven't you tried kissing our pretty cousins? I'm afraid my country cousin hasn't had much experience yet with the ladies."

Nathan flushed darkly. " I'm sure," he said haughtily, " the kind of experience you speak of is not becoming in a gentleman."

Sam threw back his head and roared.

Conversation was pleasant at the table, for Uncle Samuel's family was scholarly, and the two young cousins with their recent college degrees made the discussions the more lively. Aunt Mary's supper too was the kind over which talk was likely to flow happily. But when the meal was over and they had left the table for the pleasant living room with its glowing fire, conversation turned to politics, and at once the room became tense. Aunt Mary tried gently to turn the talk into other channels, but the men would not be diverted.

Nathan again told the story of his meeting with George Washington. The three young boys of the house hung eagerly on his words.

" He's right, absolutely right," Nathan ended with feeling. " We can't sit back and take the injustices England is dealing out to us. The first thing we know, we'll have lost all that our forefathers gained by coming here. Oppression will be as bad as it was in the old country, only our situation here will be worse because we're not even represented in Parliament."

" And what kind of situation do you think you'd be in if it weren't for England? " young Sam asked sharply.

" One infinitely better than the one we find ourselves in at present," Nathan replied instantly.

" If some of you young egotists would learn," Sam answered scornfully, " that you'd be nothing, absolutely *nothing,* without England, that you'd have no opportunities — Why, that Yale degree of yours would be utterly wasted! "

"Education's never wasted, Sam," put in their uncle.

"The Colonies aren't going to take much more from the mother country," Nathan insisted. "If it takes armed resistance to get our rights, then it's armed resistance we'll give."

"That's treason!" young Sam shouted, jumping up. "Downright treason. You're as much a subject of the king as any man living in England, and if you had sense enough to stick with him, it would pay you big dividends."

"What do you mean by that?" Uncle Samuel demanded.

Young Sam flushed. "The Crown can use educated men in the Colonies. If colonial-born, so much the better."

"Have your eye on a nice juicy plum, do you, Sam?" his uncle asked. "A governorship, perhaps? Or would you like to be a tax collector?"

"We must think of the good of all," Nathan protested. "It's not a matter to be looked at from a selfish, personal standpoint."

"You're a visionary," Sam taunted. "You'd better get down to facts."

"I'm giving you facts." Nathan was indignant. "The facts are that the Colonies have had enough of England's tyranny, and they're just about through. If they can't get justice by any other means, they're going to fight for it."

Sam laughed. "So you want to fight, do you? Well, then, you'd better join the king's army, for they'd mow down this armed resistance you talk about in a hurry. You wouldn't have time to fight if you were with the Colonials."

There was unrest in the Samuel Hale household after their Tory cousin had left. Hot words had been spoken, and the feelings of all were agitated. Aunt Mary suggested that they had better all go to bed and forget their arguments.

Nathan paced the floor of his bedroom. Young Sam, he thought, was selfish, self-seeking, and egotistical. His cousin did not care about the suffering of others in the Colonies so long as he could see his own ambitions fed.

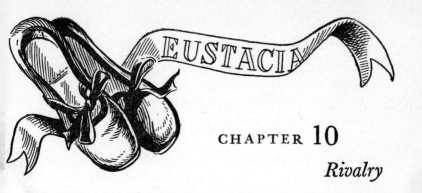

CHAPTER 10

Rivalry

BEFORE HE left Portsmouth, Nathan had secured a teaching position. A friend of his uncle, headmaster in the grammar school at East Haddam, needed a teacher and engaged him.

Carrying his credentials from Yale, Nathan set out with a light heart. He found East Haddam a picturesque little village of sleepy, quiet charm. He engaged a room at the village inn, feeling a glow of pride at being in a room wholly his, shared by no brother or college roommate, and paid for with his own money. Being independent was going to be fine. He believed he would subscribe to the penny post when he received his first wages. By paying ninepence a year, he could get fifty miles of postal carriage or, by paying eighteen, he could get one hundred miles. He would like to be able to send a letter to Coventry occasionally, and to near-by Windsor where Enoch was located, and to his Uncle Samuel.

As the weeks went on and he fell into the routine of teaching his little group of boys and girls of assorted ages, he longed more and more for Alice. Life at East Haddam was lonely after the house full of cousins he had just left and the comradeship of the fellows at Yale for the past four years. He wondered often about Alice's life with Ripley. He hoped she wasn't unhappy. Perhaps she had come to care for Ripley, for he would be good to her. There was a barb in the thought. But if by loving Ripley, Alice could find some measure of happiness, he could not begrudge it to her.

He had never taken an interest in any other girl; and even now, when Alice was definitely lost to him, his indifference to other girls prevailed. The glances of the East Haddam girls, cast from under their bonnets when their mothers were not looking, were wasted. He was pleasant to them all, smiling and bowing to them at church, but showing no inclination to single anyone out to take to singing school, to a taffy pull, or to a bobsled party. But red-haired, brown-eyed vivacious Eustacia Middlebranch, Nathan found, had an advantage. She and her parents, who had moved to East Haddam from Portsmouth, knew Uncle Samuel and his family, and Cousin Sam. Nathan found himself often invited to dine with the Middlebranches.

He suspected that there might have been a romantic attachment between Eustacia and Sam, for she spoke of him with a coquetry that did not seem to belong to a friend-of-the-family relationship.

" Nathan," she had begged him, on his first visit to her home, her big brown eyes pleading, " let's have some parties this winter and liven things up. It's frightfully dull here after Portsmouth. When you're young, you want things gay and exciting." She caught her hands above her head and twirled around on her toes. "Dance with me," she coaxed, ending up at his side, swaying with the music she hummed.

"I don't dance," Nathan told her.

"Then you'll have to learn. I'll teach you and we'll give a dancing party."

But Nathan demurred. He could not toss off his Puritan upbringing as readily as a moth casts off its cocoon. Besides, he was not anxious to become involved in plans which he suddenly began to suspect Eustacia was evolving to throw them together.

However, it was not easy to escape Eustacia. She soon learned that he liked to take long walks, and after that she hunted out his favorite paths. So he would round a bend to find her just ahead of him, very much surprised to see him; or he would come down off a steep hill path to the road, only to have her overtake him in her pony cart. She made a pretty picture, holding the lines with assurance, a bright velvet hat with a perky feather perched on her bright head, a brown velvet suit with fur trim buttoned up to her chin. There was nothing for him to do but get in and ride with her.

When he attended a spelling bee or a singing school in the evening, it became exceedingly difficult to slip out early enough to avoid Mr. Middlebranch's invitation to ride home with them. If he accepted, he found himself riding at Eustacia's side. If he made excuses he felt that he was being ungrateful.

But despite the fact that he came to enjoy Eustacia's gay company, he did not like her persistent campaign.

He had given Alice up in fact, but his heart had not yet relinquished her. He would not marry for a long time, he told himself, if ever. He would devote his efforts to finding his life's work and doing it well.

Sometimes he felt as if teaching in East Haddam were a waste of precious time from his life. Still, the boys and girls seemed to like him and learned much more than their required lessons, so he supposed he was doing some little good. He knew the boys admired his skill in athletics. They could never get enough of seeing him jump. The little girls were sweet and shy with him and brought him little things they made — pincushions, and needlecases, and even embroidered kerchiefs and knitted wristlets. One day one of the bigger girls brought him a pair of socks, and he thought with a pang of the pair Alice had knit for him and hidden in his pocket when he first left home.

Late in December came stirring news from Boston. A band of Bostonians, dressed like Indians, had boarded British ships in the harbor — ships filled with tea that the Colonies were expected to buy and on which they would have to pay threepence a pound duty — and had dumped three hundred and forty-two chests of it into the sea. That had taken courage, Nathan felt, the kind the Colonies would have to exhibit. He found himself wishing he were in Boston.

Little by little news seeped into East Haddam that Boston was not the only port that had taken a stand when ships arrived with consignments of tea. New York and Philadelphia sent ships back, their full cargoes still on board. In Charleston, although the tea was landed, it was not permitted to be sold but was stored in damp cellars to mold.

Also in December came news from Coventry that affected Nathan deeply. Alice had a son. Now, it seemed to him, she was another person — not the young girl he had known, but a woman with a child.

After that, as the weeks and months went by, he found himself turning more and more to Eustacia. He had a need for something to fill the emptiness within him. One afternoon she stopped at the schoolhouse after the last of the children had straggled away. She was just going by, she said, on an errand for her mother. It was not the first time she had thus paid him a call, and he was troubled.

" I don't think," he said, " that you should stop in here this way. People are likely to say unkind things. It isn't exactly becoming in a young girl to seem too forward."

Eustacia laughed, looking up at him audaciously. " Do you think me forward? "

" I didn't say that, Eustacia. But I'm afraid some of the townspeople might misunderstand. This isn't Portsmouth, you know."

" I used to mind that it wasn't — but that was before you came." She put her hand on his arm.

" Eustacia," he said, taking hold of her arms. Suddenly, they both turned, sensing another presence. In the door stood young Sam Hale.

" Well, my friends! " he greeted them, a biting note of sarcasm in his tone.

" Oh, it's you, Sam," Eustacia said, completely at

ease. " Mother and father will be glad to see you. Nathan, you must come to supper with us. We'll have a party afterward."

Sam set his lips together unpleasantly, but said nothing.

" Come on." She put a hand through an arm of each of the young men. " We'll all go downtown and do the errand mother sent me on."

The three of them set out for town — the spirited, pretty girl, her red head held high and her full, sprigged muslin skirts trailing the brick sidewalk behind her; the dark, handsome Sam, a little sullen now, tall and straight on her right; light-haired, fine-featured Nathan, tall and straight on her left. Nathan's eyes held a quickly conceived mischief. He had determined to show his cousin that he was not, after all, such a dud with the girls.

He became his most charming self, bowing and smiling at acquaintances they met, being deferential to Eustacia. Eustacia laughed up at him and squeezed his arm. Suddenly, a little pang of conscience stabbed him. What if Eustacia took him seriously? But still, what if she did? he thought recklessly. There would be worse girls a young chap could marry. Eustacia was gay and pretty; she was clever and intelligent. She could be a very enjoyable companion, and she would be a social asset to any young man who wanted to get ahead.

Nathan dressed for the evening with care, recalling that he had dressed as carefully the night Sam had come to dine at Uncle Samuel's. That evening had driven in the entering wedge between him and Sam — first the episode of their pretty cousins, then the matter of politics. Now there was Eustacia.

Supper was gay. The candles on the table gave a mellow luster to the heavy damask cloth and to the old silver which Mrs. Middlebranch's grandmother had brought over from England as a bride.

" Eustacia is to have it when she marries," Mrs. Middlebranch ended her account of the silver. " She will be the fourth generation to start housekeeping with it."

" It reminds me of the beautiful silverware I saw in a shop in Boston," Nathan said. " Perhaps you know the shop, Sam. The silversmith's name is Paul Revere."

" Yes, I've heard of it."

" I just couldn't leave Boston without buying a few pieces of his silver. It was exquisite."

" Starting a dowry? I thought that was woman's sphere," Sam said unpleasantly.

Nathan smiled. " I brought Aunt Mary a piece and saved another piece for a gift." He had resolved to have no arguments with his cousin at the Middlebranches'; nevertheless, he was going to show him some competition with Eustacia. She was sitting between them, sparkling with high spirits, and Nathan smiled at how adroitly she was playing the Hale cousins against each other.

" What are you doing for music? " Sam asked.

" Music? " Eustacia repeated absently.

" For the party tonight."

" We're not having music. We're going to play games."

" You mean we're not going to dance? "

"No. Nathan doesn't dance."

Sam was more than annoyed. "But perhaps the rest of us do, and Nathan might learn."

"No," she said decisively. "Nathan doesn't care to learn, and I don't care so much about it myself. We'll play games instead. They're lots of fun."

The games, once they started, went on and on. Nathan enjoyed the fun and enjoyed Sam's angry impatience. Finally, as he stood with Eustacia, who was flushed and breathless from the last game, his cousin approached.

"Let's step outside for a look at the moon," Sam suggested to the girl, ignoring Nathan.

"I'm afraid Eustacia would catch cold," Nathan said. "It's warm in here."

Eustacia flashed Nathan a smile. "I guess I'd better not, Sam."

The next game started, and Nathan whisked Eustacia away, leaving Sam standing alone. But instead of entering into the game, Nathan drew Eustacia into the dining room.

"Eustacia," he said. Then he hesitated. Was this, after all, what he wanted? He would never again find anyone like Alice, he supposed; yet a fellow had to have a wife. "I haven't had a chance to speak to your father," he went on. "I suppose I should, before I say anything to you. If it's agreeable to you, though, I'll see him tomorrow."

"If what's agreeable to me?" Her hair touched his face as she spoke.

"If you think I'd be all right — as a husband. We

probably won't live here. I may secure a position in New London . . . "

" Nathan! " Eustacia cried without hearing him out. Her voice told him enough.

By degrees the guests took their leave. Finally only the two Hale cousins were left.

" It's late," Nathan said at last. " I guess we'd better be going, Sam. In the morning, I'll take care of that matter we were discussing, Eustacia." He started toward the door, but Sam made no move to follow.

" I believe I'll stay for a little while, Nathan," he said. " After all, I *did* come to see Eustacia, and so far " — pointedly — " I haven't had much chance."

Nathan looked questioningly at Eustacia.

Eustacia, as usual, had the situation instantly in hand.

" I don't believe you'd better, Sam," she said. " Perhaps I should tell you something, so you'll understand. Nathan and I are engaged."

Sam's face went through a series of lightning changes — amazement, incredulity, anger. Then, without a word, he grabbed his hat and strode from the room, slamming the door behind him like a child in a tantrum.

A month before Nathan left East Haddam to assume new teaching duties as preceptor of the Union Grammar School in New London, a newcomer took up residence at the inn. He was a dashing young fellow, whose laugh rang through the halls as he came and went about his business. The first night he was in town, he announced that he was going to start a shoe store. This news caused great excitement. To be able to try on shoes before buying them was unheard of; East Haddam's shoes were ordered from Boston — sight unseen and fit untried.

It seemed to Nathan that the young man's choice of a business and of a location was scarcely an exhibition of sound judgment, but he confided that his father had plenty of money to establish him. He dressed handsomely in the bright satin frock coat and breeches of a gentleman — a sight indeed for homespun East Haddam. His name was Trevor Merriweather.

Eustacia and Nathan were out walking when they first saw him. He came tearing into town like a whirlwind, astride a handsome, dapple-gray horse, leaving a trail of dust hanging over the street. Eustacia stared, her mouth and eyes open wide.

" Who do you suppose he could be? " she asked excitedly.

" A wild Indian, from the way he rides," Nathan said.

" Did you see the way he was dressed? "

" Yes; it would take an Indian brave to get those colors together."

" Nathan, you're joking! Oh, I do wonder who he is and what he's doing in East Haddam! "

The next time Nathan saw Eustacia, she told him that she was dying to meet the town's new businessman. Did Nathan suppose he would carry shoes small enough for her feet? Nathan smiled at her vanity and assured her that Mr. Merriweather would carry ladies' shoes, and that he would certainly have some small sizes.

" Then I hope he'll have some red ones," Eustacia cried. " I'm simply dying for some red dancing slippers."

Nathan raised an eyebrow. Was this the Eustacia who had given up dancing?

The stranger had such a romantic-sounding name, she went on — Trevor Merriweather. Why, it was like a song, or a poem. He was handsome too, and just think of anyone in East Haddam dressing so elegantly!

Nathan promised her that he would get her an introduction to Mr. Merriweather. The opportunity came shortly. He was walking down Main Street with Eustacia after school when a flash of color darted out of the inn and dashed down the thoroughfare toward them. The rainbow was Merriweather, on his way to the store he was getting ready. He stopped in his tracks, removed his hat in a sweeping bow, and came up with a wide smile as Nathan made the introduction.

" I'm charmed," he said to Eustacia. Then, with a flash of white teeth at Nathan, " So you, my friend, are the fortunate one who strolls with the town's most beautiful lady! "

They chatted a few moments before going their respective ways.

" O Nathan," Eustacia sighed, almost before Merriweather was out of earshot, " isn't he wonderful? "

Nathan looked sideways at her.

" When do you want him for supper? " he asked dryly.

The supper reminded Nathan of the one at the Middlebranches' when his cousin Sam Hale had been the extra guest. Now he was playing that part, and he found that he did not care. He saw through Eustacia's maneuvers plainly. He caught Mrs. Middlebranch glancing at him anxiously.

For a few days following the supper party, he watched Eustacia flit excitedly back and forth between him and Merriweather. She was not at ease, however — more, Nathan thought, for fear he would tell Merriweather of their engagement than for fear she would hurt him. He would let her struggle a little longer, he decided. He would be leaving East Haddam soon, and the idea of being Eustacia's " jilted " lover in the eyes of the townspeople did not bother him. He would chalk this brief engagement up to experience and, perhaps, be wiser in his understanding of human nature.

Eustacia was quick to agree when he suggested that she break the engagement. He scarcely saw her after that, but he understood that she was very busy in her new red slippers, dancing in the satin-clad arms of young Merriweather.

CHAPTER 11

Armed Resistance

NATHAN, JOURNEYING from
East Haddam to New London, wondered whether he
should not give up all ideas of turning to some other
line of work after a year or two of teaching, for the
" other work " was still intangible and undefined. He
could probably do as much good training boys for Yale
and giving girls some of the education he thought they
should have as he could doing anything else. At New
London, he was to give the girls instruction in the
mornings from five o'clock to seven, before the regular
school day began. Teaching didn't take courage, but
perhaps his dream of a job requiring courage was
childish. He would give the boys and girls in New
London what inspiration he could. He would try to
show them that they were living in stirring times and
that they must develop into men and women strong
enough to meet the challenge of their age.

So he took up his second year of teaching with enthusiasm, and the contagion of it spread to his pupils.
He and his boys soon were a close-knit band of patriots,
fired with a common zeal for justice to the Colonies.
Each morning they prayed earnestly together before

beginning the day's lessons, and each evening when classes were over, they discussed what the Colonies should do.

" I met George Washington once," Nathan told the boys.

Excited exclamations greeted this news. They had been studying Washington's part in the French and Indian War and knew he had been the commander of the Virginia troops.

" He told me," Nathan went on, " that in the end we'd have to resort to armed resistance."

Samuel Green, one of the boys, leaned on the teacher's desk. " Then we ought to be training this very minute. Let's organize a company. Will you drill us, Mr. Hale? "

" I don't know how your parents would feel about it," Nathan answered. " They might think I was stirring up sedition."

" But we'd form the company ourselves — only those who wanted to join."

" And that would be all of us," one of the boys cried.

" That's right," cried another. " Come on; let's do it! "

" We'll think about it," Nathan agreed. " Perhaps we should be thought a little premature if we started drilling now." Then, seeing their disappointment, he added, " At least if we started tonight."

The boys went trooping noisily out.

Nathan checked the sums on the slates which were piled high on one end of his desk, and swept the floor. Then he straightened the shades, gave one last glance about the room, and turned the key in the lock. He was still preoccupied, as he started homeward, with thoughts of forming a company that might someday be of aid to the Colonies. He liked living in a private home as he was doing this year. He found that he needed the wholesome, companionable feeling of a home. He could afford to live well now, for, with the seventy pounds which he received as salary and the additional money he made from tutoring in the evenings, he had a neat income. He had a pleasant room in the home of a family named Richards and was made to feel one of them.

As he approached the house, he saw Mrs. Richards waiting for him at the door with a letter.

He hoped it was real news. He found himself constantly on the alert these days for word of the political situation. Something was going to happen on this side of the water if England didn't change her tactics; of that he was positive. The Colonies were aroused anew over having to house and feed British regulars stationed in their midst, and they were not satisfied with England's argument that since the soldiers had been sent over to help the Colonies in the French and Indian War, it was no more than right that the Colonies should support them.

He had heard that Samuel Adams had established a Committee of Correspondence for interchanging the ideas and plans of the Colonies' leading citizens, hoping to develop a united spirit. This was the Samuel Adams whom the old man in Boston had told him about when he was en route to Portsmouth following graduation. He thought Adams' plan was a good one, and felt that it would unite the Colonies in action as well as in thought.

The letter Mrs. Richards handed him was addressed in his father's hand, and there was the mark of the penny post in the corner. He was surprised, both at seeing a letter from the Deacon and at seeing that he was using the penny post.

" Thank you," he said, taking the letter and starting toward the stairs. Going up the steps, he felt an uneasy premonition, and his hand was not quite steady as he closed the door to his room and ripped open the envelope. There was one page in the Deacon's large script.

" Dear Son," the letter began, " we have sad news to impart to you."

Nathan, scanning the lines quickly, caught Alice's name. Had they let something happen to her? He felt a tightness in his throat.

" Alice has been left a widow," he read. " Elijah died of pneumonia the twenty-sixth day of December and was buried on the twenty-eighth in the family lot at Coventry. Never a finer young man lived. His death is a great loss to the community as well as to all of us and to Alice. Alice has come back home with the baby — "

Nathan stopped. Alice running about the kitchen again, helping Martha dip up the beans, laughing — But no — there would be no laughter. She was a widow now, wearing sober black and caring for her child.

He read the rest of the letter. Abigail wasn't well this winter, so she could use Alice's help. Couldn't Nathan come home when his term at New London was over? It had been so long since they had seen him.

Nathan wondered. Was his father thinking of how he had separated him and Alice? Was he hoping now to throw them together since Alice was without means of support? He did not know. This was February. The New London term would be out in June. He counted the months from Ripley's death till June. Six months. Would that be too soon? Would Alice want him to come? He felt a strange depression, a foreboding. But a foreboding of what? He did not know, unless it came from a fear that Alice, after her experience of wifehood and motherhood and widowhood, would be so changed that the old Alice would be only a dream he had cherished in a deep corner of his heart. Or perhaps the feeling came from a fear that Alice would no longer care for him. Maybe her feeling had been only a girlish fancy. After all, she had married Ripley instead of waiting for him. He gave up pondering and went downstairs to supper.

" Bad news from home? " Mrs. Richards asked when she saw his troubled face.

" My brother-in-law died last month," he said. Until this moment, he had never thought of Ripley as his brother-in-law. Perhaps he would go home when the term was out, he decided as he sat down to a meal of spareribs. Mrs. Richards was a good cook, but how he would like some of Abigail's baked beans and hot buns! And Abigail had not been well, his father said. Yes; he must go home.

But he was not to go home as he planned. As spring came on, he finally gave in and organized his boys into a zealous little company which drilled for two hours each night after school. If they accomplished nothing else, he thought, they developed a military carriage and became familiar with the simpler commands.

On a night in April, as they were marching down the dusty road in front of the schoolhouse, to the rhythm of Nathan's "Hep! Hep! Hep!", clubs over their shoulders in lieu of guns, a horse and rider approached at great speed.

Nathan obliqued his company to the side of the road. As the rider passed in a billow of dust, he lifted his hat and called to them. Over the thunder of the rapid hoof-beats they caught only a part of what he said.

"There's been fighting!"

"Did he say at Lexington?" Nathan demanded.

The little company broke ranks and stood staring after the rider as he galloped into the village. A dozen voices tried to answer at once.

"Concord."

"No, Lexington."

"I thought he said Lexington *and* Concord."

"There's been fighting. I heard that."

"Maybe we'll get to go — "

"Attention!" Nathan commanded. His face was grave as he looked at his reassembled company of eager boys. "This probably means war," he said. "Let us proceed at once to get the news in full. Forward, march!"

In double-quick time they entered the village square where citizens were gathering about the messenger. Nathan edged his way toward the center of the crowd.

"What is it?" he asked a tall, rawboned fellow who

had evidently learned the news and was now elbowing
his way back to the edge of the crowd.

" They've defied the redcoats at Lexington and Concord."

" What happened? "

" Don't know. A few got killed."

" But what started it? "

" They were after the ammunition at Concord,"
someone replied.

" Hancock and Sam Adams," Nathan caught from
the confused turmoil of voices.

" What about Hancock and Adams? " he demanded,
working his way still nearer the messenger.

" They were going to arrest them," the messenger
answered.

" Did they? "

" No; they were challenged by Captain Parker and
about sixty men at Lexington."

" And there was fighting? "

" Yes, sir! The British fired first — "

" What about Concord? "

" There was fighting there too. Four hundred farmers met them at a bridge outside the town."

" Four hundred? "

' " And how the redcoats ran! "

" You don't mean to say they retreated? "

" Retreated? They were routed. Why, man, we heard
they lost three hundred men! "

" Three hundred? How many were there to start
with? "

" Nearly a thousand."

" And four hundred farmers — "

" Four hundred farmers, yes. They chased the British clear across Charlestown Neck till they were safe under the guns of their own vessels."

" Four hundred farmers! " Nathan exclaimed. His eyes were points of fire. " But how did they know the regulars were coming? "

" Paul Revere — "

" Paul Revere? Not the silversmith in Boston? "

" The same. He started out at eleven o'clock at night and rode like mad, waking the farmers along the way, warning the countryside that the redcoats were coming."

Goose flesh came out on Nathan's body. Paul Revere! He had visited his shop in Boston; from him he had bought the spoons for Abigail and Aunt Mary. Paul Revere, riding alone though the night and rousing four hundred men to rout the British in the Colonies' first attempt at armed resistance!

" There'll be a town meeting at twilight," one of the town's aldermen — Alderman Brown by name — called to Nathan as the crowd began to disperse. The messenger had mounted and had ridden on to fire other towns with his report. " At Miner's Tavern. We'll expect to see you there."

Nathan made his way back toward the schoolhouse. He walked with his hands deep in his pockets and his head down, not seeing the soft billows of clean, fresh green which the new-leafed trees made against the sky, nor feeling the caress of the spring wind in his hair, nor hearing the chirping of early nesting birds. He had known instantly, upon learning the news, what he must do. Now his mind ran a double course.

With one part of it he made plans. He would ask leave from his school, or simply resign. He could get things in shape at the schoolhouse tonight. He would like to meet his boys once more. He could call school as usual in the morning, but dismiss early. He would have to send a letter to his father at Coventry to let him know of his move.

Another part of his mind went over the story the messenger had brought. Paul Revere's ride; the little band of sixty men under young Captain Parker, standing in the face of the measured approach of a thousand redcoats; four hundred farmers, shooting from behind stone walls into that military pattern of red and gold and breaking it into disorder and chaos. His mind went beyond this and saw something of what it would mean tomorrow, and the next day, and the next. Untrained soldiers fighting against a military machine; unequipped men against men well armed. The Colonies must organize. They must start making munitions. They had shown at Concord what courage and conviction could do. But more than courage and conviction would be required in the days to come.

When he reached Miner's Tavern that night, a hundred or so men were already there. Some had heard one thing, some another. But Nathan's interest lay in what they were going to do.

" Who's to be in charge of the meeting? " he asked Mr. Green, the father of one of his pupils.

" I don't know, Mr. Hale. I ain't heard."

Nathan went from group to group, asking the same question and getting the same reply. Apparently no one was in charge. The men continued their discussions in shifting groups.

" So it's agonna be war after all. I'd a never believed we'd a lived t'see it come — not war agin' our mother country," an old farmer said as Nathan edged to the group in which he was standing.

" Why not? " Nathan asked. " We've tried everything else to get our rights. They only ignore us, or pass more stringent rules. Look at the Port Bill, the Quartering Acts — "

" What's them? " the farmer inquired out of the side of a tobacco-filled mouth.

Nathan began to explain. The group about him drew closer. Others edged in.

" Why don't you get up on a table and tell us all, schoolmaster? " Mr. Green asked.

Nathan hesitated.

" Go on. Go ahead. Tell us," others urged.

Nathan's hesitation lasted only a moment. After all, someone had to take charge. What could they hope to accomplish standing about like this, hashing over the details of the afternoon's news, doing nothing? He leaped upon one of the crude, wooden tables and clapped his hands together for attention.

" Gentlemen! Gentlemen! "

The groups turned toward him and ceased talking.

" Gentlemen," he began when the room had quieted, " we have all heard the account of the messenger from Concord. This is not, sirs, an incident belonging to

Lexington and Concord alone. It is, rather, proof that the controversy that has been raging between us and England must be settled by arms. If we must wage war, let it be war for a permanent good. The torch of armed conflict has already been lighted. Let us carry it high and far, far enough to gain a lasting independence. I say, gentlemen, let us march immediately, and not lay down our arms until we have obtained independence."

Pandemonium broke out in the room.

" He's right! He's right! "

" Independence! "

Nathan saw he had struck the match that would set off the smoldering uncertainty in their minds. Content with what he had accomplished, he slipped out. The meeting no longer needed him. It was a relief to be out in the fresh evening air of spring. Something about it as it touched his cheek made him think of Alice again. Strange, he thought, when his mind was so full of what he must do, and of what the Colonies must do, of a man's world, that thoughts of Alice should persist. He would not be going home in June as he had planned. Would he ever see her again?

He went to the three directors of the New London Union Grammar School and told them of his decision. They asked only that he take leave of absence rather than resign, in case he should find it possible to return.

He went home and gathered together his things, told the awe-struck Mrs. Richards what he intended to do, then went back to walk the streets restlessly, knowing that he could not sleep. He turned toward Miner's Tavern, wondering vaguely what had come of the meeting after he had left. But before he reached the tavern, he met a group of excited young men. Recognizing him, they drew him into their midst.

" We're joining up tomorrow," they told him, all talking at once. " You'll be going too, of course."

" Fine! " Nathan said. So his words had brought some immediate action. " I was planning on going down to Cambridge tomorrow. We can all go together."

The next morning, from his high teacher's desk, he faced a solemn group of boys. He said quietly, as he had said to them each morning, " Let us pray."

They knelt beside their benches, he by the chair at his desk.

" Dear God," he prayed earnestly, " give us the wisdom to meet this critical situation in the way that is best; give us courage to uphold the right, no matter what the odds against it; give us faith to know that Thou art ever with us. And so lead us out of the perilous night into the day. We thank Thee for giving us this land for freedom. Give us the strength to keep it so that we may worship Thee as we see fit and live as we believe it right to live. Give to every boy here, and to every other boy in the nation, the vision to go forward in the way Thou wouldst have him go. In Thy name we ask it. Amen."

When the noise of twenty scrambling pairs of feet had died down, and the boys were quiet, Nathan said to them: " You heard the news the messenger brought from Concord. You know what it means. The brave men at Lexington and Concord have only begun what we must take up and finish. We will be fighting for the great and noble cause of liberty."

A cheer went up from the boys.

" I will go today to do what I can for this cause. You and others will follow tomorrow — upon whatever tomorrow you are ready. Remember that your country needs trained men, educated men, the kind of men you will be if you remain a little longer in training. This will be a great country someday, our own country, and you and I will have helped to make it so. One thing only I would admonish you: Be brave and always do, to the best of your ability, the task that lies before you. Good-by, and God bless you."

CHAPTER 12

Two Captains

NATHAN HAD much to think
about as he rode through the pleasant countryside that
summer of 1775, recruiting for the American Army.
He had much to say too on occasion. When the sleepy
New England villagers seemed indifferent to the cause
that was so vital to him, he roused them with fiery
speeches.

" Do you want to be serfs? slaves? vassals? No? Then
to arms, men! To arms! "

And to the bewhiskered farmers, who were loath to
leave their crops unharvested, he talked long and earnestly.

" Those who can't fight will have to tend our fields,"
he said to them. " For if you and I and the rest of the
able-bodied men don't fight, we'll have no fields to call
our own."

Mile after mile he jogged the country roads, his own
thoughts his only companions. He felt sure the Colonies would succeed in their struggle. The foundation
of his whole philosophy was a belief in ultimate justice,
a belief that right would prevail.

He was elated, not surprised, when the news came of

Benedict Arnold and Ethan Allen's capture of Ticonderoga, of the splendid fight the Americans made at Bunker Hill, so confounding the British that they changed command from General Gage to General Howe better to meet the unforeseen strength and strategy of the Provincials. And he felt that the Second Continental Congress, in naming George Washington Commander in Chief of the American Army, had made a masterly move.

He thrilled to the further news that Washington had refused to accept compensation for his service and that he had expressed himself as feeling inadequate to the great responsibility placed upon him. He encountered many who thought this last was only a becoming evidence of modesty; but, believing that he knew Washington from his memorable encounter with him at The Happy Warrior, he did not agree.

" He really meant it," he told meeting after meeting. " I'm sure of it. He's completely honest; he would be just as honest in judging himself as in anything else. Anyone who wasn't an egotist would feel himself inadequate in the face of the job Washington has been given."

On September 1, a letter from Coventry, dated July 20, caught up with him. This was the first word he had received from home since he had written his father that he was leaving New London for Cambridge to enlist. He tore open the envelope eagerly, hoping for news of Alice. He had expected to see her long before this. Much of the letter was about Alice, but it was not the kind of news for which he had been hoping.

" Alice has had another great sorrow," the letter said, " and cannot this time seem to bear up under the crushing blow. On July 1, her baby died, and we laid him to rest beside his father on July 4. It was very sudden, and at first Alice seemed stunned and unable to take in what had happened. Then at the funeral she collapsed, and since that time she has not regained her normal state in any degree, either physically or mentally. Her mother worries greatly about her, for she does not eat and is very pale and weak. We are all much concerned over her, but hope that she will soon show improvement."

Nathan's heart ached at the thought of Alice slipping about the house like a ghost, gone the joy and laughter that had been her very nature. He longed to go to her, but there was no chance of that. He was now a soldier, and not a part-time soldier like some of these young fellows who had deserted as soon as they found they could not be in the Army and still go home every night. He was enrolled for as long as his country needed him.

At least he could write to Alice about some of his experiences in visiting the farms and villages. Perhaps if he could make her realize that others too had sorrows, but picked up and went on — There was the Munson family, for instance, whom he had visited the week before. They had lost three sons within the year, all of the same disease, and knew that it would not be long before they would lose a fourth. Yet they went about their work of making the home warm and happy for the children that were left. He wished he had the ability to make Alice see Mrs. Munson. He would carry a mental picture of her as long as he lived. She was beautiful, sweet-faced and serene, instead of warped and bitter. He would try to find words to picture her for Alice.

In September he was called in from his recruiting expedition and commissioned a captain. At headquarters he found his old friend Hull, who had been made a captain in the same regiment. The regiment was commanded by Colonel Webb. Nothing could be finer, Nathan thought, than this opportunity to renew his friendship with Hull.

Then the Connecticut troops were ordered to Boston. In conjunction with the Massachusetts troops, it would be their task to keep the British cooped up in that city. Nathan was glad of the move. This would seem more like active service.

But when Colonel Webb's regiment arrived on the bare hill that was to be their campgrounds, he found it difficult to muster much enthusiasm. They would have to establish winter quarters, and there was little to do this with. Tents? Huts? Which should they attempt? He and Hull went out to reconnoiter. Sails were being brought from the port towns from which some tents could be made, but these would not go far. There was plenty of timber and brush on the hills about. Could they build with this? The men were set to work cutting timber, making tent poles, chopping wood for fuel.

The huts went up slowly. Some of the soldiers tried cutting sod into blocks and using them for building stones. Putting up shelter for the seven thousand men who were to spend the winter on that bleak hill was a long and tedious job; long before there were accommodations for all, the air had turned chill and the snow had begun to fly. " Camp Winter Hill," the men called their encampment. At near-by Roxbury was a similar camp. Together the two camps served their purpose of imprisoning the British in the city. When the shelters were finally finished, what was there left to do?

Nathan drilled his company long and hard, but still there were many idle hours through the long days and nights. The men grew homesick and were ill content with their poor shelters as the cold increased in bitterness. Casting about in his mind for something to interest his men and improve their morale, Nathan suggested to his company that they adopt a uniform.

They couldn't afford to buy uniforms, they replied dismally.

" Uniforms need be no more expensive," Nathan argued, " than the clothes you're wearing. You'll feel so much more like an army. It's demoralizing to go straggling like farmers and tradesmen. We don't feel like soldiers."

He won his point, and the first uniformed company on Winter Hill went strutting about as proud as little boys with new Christmas trappings. The uniform was simple enough: a long, fringed shirt, belted in at the waist, and leggings, fastened just above the shoe tops. But it had something of the effect he had hoped for. Other companies decided they would not be outdone. Little by little the hill took on a semblance of uniformity when the men were at drill.

But the improved morale was short-lived. The six

months' period for which the men had enlisted was fast drawing to a close, and to Nathan it was evident that many had no intention of re-enlisting. Imprisoning the British in Boston was all that could be hoped for as Washington lacked ammunition to attack and drive them out. The situation was serious, and, to make it worse, the soldiers' pay was becoming increasingly irregular. December arrived, and they had not been paid since early fall.

"It's a shame they haven't been paid," Hull said. "If they had a little money in their pockets, they could buy things they need that we can't furnish them. Their food could stand to be supplemented. And they could get warmer socks and mittens, and tobacco for their pipes."

"Why can't they see that the cause is more important than their personal wants?" Nathan broke in impatiently.

"Remember," said Hull, "it's not as if they were fighting, not as if they could see that they were doing something."

After Hull had gone to his own tent, Nathan lay rolled in his blankets, none too warm, thinking. Perhaps if he held his company together, other companies would follow, as they had done with the uniforms. He would talk to his men tomorrow. He planned carefully what he would say, for he wanted first of all to impress them with the necessity for a unified, drilled army for Washington to use when the time was ripe. He wanted to make them feel the greatness of Washington as he himself felt it, wanted them to put their trust in the commander. And he had to renew their enthusiasm for gaining independence, for it had lagged woefully since they had discovered that the job was not to be done in a moment, that it was something that involved hunger and cold and hardship, waiting through interminable winter months, and going without pay.

He got up and stirred the fire, pulled his blankets about him, and sat hunched by the little blaze. What could he do to hold them? Money? Money, as Hull had said, was probably the thing. If only he had the money, he'd pay them out of his own pocket. But of course he did not have enough. He continued to ponder the problem into the gray winter dawn.

By the time he took his men for drill, he had determined upon his course.

" Attention! " he called.

The company responded as one man. At least, he thought, they had learned to take commands and act like soldiers.

" Men," he said, " I realize that talk of loyalty isn't what you want. You know the necessity of our remaining here at Washington's command as well as I do. I met George Washington once, and I know that whatever he commands is the right and only thing for us to do. Though you know you're needed, personal considerations make you forget how important it is that you stay on. You want your pay. You want money to buy things for your wives and sweethearts. You want money to send to your families. You want money to buy things for yourselves — mufflers, perhaps, to keep out this bitter wind. I understand that. I know you want it and

should have it. So you're going to get your back pay —
now, before you are dismissed. I determined last night
to make up what I could of your wages out of my own
pocket, but — " with a wry smile — " my pockets
didn't yield enough to go around. So I have given my
note, with my advance pay as security, and have bor-
rowed the additional cash to pay you in full."

Every man in Nathan's company re-enlisted. The
example they set had a wholesome effect on the re-en-
listments of Webb's entire regiment.

Nathan felt that at last, perhaps, he had done some
small bit toward living up to Washington's faith in him.
" It's men like you that will throw off the yoke of tyranny Britain is imposing on the Colonies," Washington had said. Time and again, the words had come back
to him since that day at The Happy Warrior.

CHAPTER 13

Reawakening

IN LATE December, Nathan received his first leave. The distance from Boston to New Haven seemed much greater than in the early autumn of 1773 when he had traveled it the other way to visit his uncle in Portsmouth. After New Haven, there was still the day's ride to Coventry, but he had decided to stop over at Yale. He found President Daggett and most of his professors still on the campus, but few students that he knew. The boys were drilling in the college yard where he and Tallmadge and Hull had played at racing and jumping. The name of Benedict Arnold was much on the tongues of the New Haven folk, for hadn't he gone out and recruited his own men and led them to Ticonderoga — he and Ethan Allen, whom he had met along the way? And then hadn't they gone on to capture Crown Point, securing much-needed arms and ammunition for the American troops about Boston?

It seemed to Nathan that for a time he again became Hale Secundus. Passing familiar landmarks on the way to Coventry, he thought of his first home-coming from Yale. Then the family had expected him. Now no one

knew he was coming. Then he had been away from
home for only a year; this time it was three years. Then
all his feelings had been one pin point of anticipation;
now his emotions were confused. There was an uncertainty, almost a dread, in the thought of seeing Alice.
He had written her twice, but had received no reply,
and what the Deacon had written was not encouraging.
Nor were Nathan's feelings about the rest of the family
settled or sure. The three younger boys, who had still
been children when he left, would now be young men.
Would he seem a stranger to them? Would they seem
strangers to him? And what of his father? The anger he
had felt at the Deacon when Alice was married had
long since died. But still he could not help remembering what his father's highhandedness had done to
Alice's life. Did the Deacon think of that too? And
would the thought be a barrier between them? Only
about Abigail did it seem to him that his feelings were
unchanged and untroubled.

The dark came early, blotting out the landscape.
Nothing of the rolling hills, the orchard, or the sugar-
maple grove was distinguishable when he turned into
the lane. But the friendly squares of light that marked
the windows of the house, and the familiar direction
the lane took, and something about the smell of the air
— What was it? The barn? Didn't all barns smell alike?
The wood smoke from the chimneys of the house? The
pine tree that he had brushed in passing? It must be all
of them, he thought, combined in a tang that had
meant Hale farm in winter to a little boy, to a gangly
adolescent, and that meant home to him now.

Abigail's eyes were bright as she held out her arms to him. The Deacon received him with respect, and, for the first time in his life, he found his father talking to him as to an equal. John and the younger boys undisguisedly looked up to him. Evidently the news that he had been made a captain had greatly impressed all the family except Alice, to whom no news seemed to matter.

Alice had smiled at him and had said, " Nathan! " in a slightly surprised, pleased tone. He had gone to her and taken both of her cold hands in his, and she had looked into his eyes as if searching hopelessly for an answer to a question that she already knew to be unanswerable. He had not realized how pitiful she would be. She made him think of a lost lamb he had picked up once when he was a small boy; her eyes held that same helpless, pleading look. All the brightness had gone out of her. Even her hair, which had always been lustrous, was dull and drab. He tried to think of some way to help her.

When he wakened the next morning, his thoughts were at once of the nook where he and Alice had met as children. His impulse was to leap out of bed and follow the path to the barn, jump the wall, and race the short distance down the lane to the nook. But he looked out of the window to see a world all white. It had snowed during the night, and the sky seemed as white as the land, so that there was no discernible break at the horizon. The only spot of color was the red barn. The pine trees looked like towering white cones, tipped with green, and the back fence posts had on dunce caps. He'd show Alice the dunce caps from the kitchen window.

Alice smiled faintly when he led her to the window and pointed out his discovery.

"But dunce caps don't mean as much to you as to me," he said, when he saw how unsuccessful his attempt to interest her had been. "I had to use them on my little folks at East Haddam when they didn't pay attention to what I was saying. Alice, you're not paying attention to what I'm saying either. I'll have to make you a dunce cap." He lifted her chin in his hand. "Chin up," he said. "That's part of what I've been drilling into everyone, first my boys at New London, and then my men at camp, and I guess I'll have to start on you."

But it was no good. She only looked at him with sad eyes.

After breakfast the insistent thought of the secret nook came to him again.

"Alice," he said impulsively, "put on your coat and bonnet and come out with me, won't you?"

"Why, Nathan?" she asked.

"Oh, I'd like to have a walk, and I want company. I miss Enoch. I'm not used to having him away preaching when I'm at home."

Obediently, but without interest, Alice put on her coat and bonnet and let Nathan pull on her boots. She did not ask where they were going when he led her toward the barn, then through the gate, and on into the unbroken snow of the pasture beyond. The air was still, and warm for January.

" Look! The corncrib with father's yellow corn in it looks like a peach cobbler," he said, trying again to interest her.

She rewarded him with the faintest trace of a smile.

He stopped when they reached the top of the bank that formed the near edge of the nook. Alice looked up at him questioningly.

" Stay here a second," he said, and slipped down over the bank in a flutter of snow. " Now jump! " As submissively as she did everything, she jumped into his arms.

" Look! " he commanded her. The bushes that surrounded the spot on three sides, piled with snow, could have been white rocks along a shore.

" We've never seen it like this before, have we? " he said. He searched her face. " How did it look when we used to come in the spring, or summer, or fall? I can hardly remember." How well he remembered every detail of it in every season!

She seemed to be making an effort to focus her mind on what he had said, but she did not reply.

" How did it look, Alice, that first time I brought you to it when we were — How old were we? Fourteen? "

" Beautiful," she said softly. " It always looked beautiful."

Nathan's heart skipped a beat. Had his impulse to bring her here been heaven-sent?

" Do you remember the last time that we were here? " he ventured.

She raised her eyes to his, and for the first time the

veil that had lain heavily over them lifted.

" Of course, Nathan! "

He took her in his arms, and suddenly she began to sob. He pulled a handkerchief from his pocket and wiped the tears from her face.

" They might freeze," he said, smiling at her. She smiled a little too, tremulously, then turned back to put her head on his shoulder. He patted her gently and let her cry.

" That's what you should have done long ago," he said when she had grown quieter. " I should have been here, but I couldn't come."

" O Nathan," she said piteously, " he was such a beautiful baby. It was so wonderful to feel his little head cuddled against my neck."

" Go on, Alice. Tell me about him."

" He had hair the color of the sun, and his big blue eyes would twinkle up at me just as if he knew I was laughing at him."

She seemed to gain strength from him. He held her tenderly, thinking that the love he felt for her now was finer and deeper and more sustaining than that which he had known the last time they had been together.

" Alice," he said at last, " I'm afraid you'll get too cold if we stay out longer — "

" I'm warm, Nathan," she answered, " warmer than I've been since baby died."

Nathan sighed in relief. " Then I'm never going to let you go," he whispered. " You'll never again be lonely, or afraid, or cold."

Nathan was at home all of January. When the time

came for him to go back to duty, he was content.

There had been no trouble this time to get a few moments alone with Alice by the fire. In fact, on his last evening, he had caught the Deacon clearing his throat and motioning Abigail toward the stairs. That night the clock on the mantel ticked off the minutes all too fast. It was hard to part from Alice because he had no idea how long they would be separated after this furlough was ended.

" As soon as the war is over," he said, " we'll build our own home, in our own country — not England's country, but *ours*."

They stood before the dying fire, loath to say good night. He saw that Alice's eyes rested on the coat of arms over the mantel.

" It's always meant a great deal to you, hasn't it? " she asked. " Tell me about it."

" I've always thought it stood for a very special kind of courage. When I was a small boy, I used to try to think of deeds that would require such courage."

" What kind of deeds, Nathan? "

" Oh, I remember I used to think about Oliver Cromwell defying the divine right of kings. I dreamed of doing something like that myself someday — something worthy of the coat of arms."

" But you are! You're helping to free people from tyranny."

" It's such a little help, Alice. I drill a hundred men."

" And keep them from deserting. That seems to me to take a special kind of courage."

Nathan laughed, cupped her chin in his hand, and

raised her face so that her eyes looked into his. " I like you when you talk like that."

Alice did not laugh with him. "*I* need courage, Nathan."

He took her hands again. " Take the coat of arms for yours too," he said.

When he went back to Winter Hill, he took eleven recruits with him, among them Asher Wright, whom he hoped to have as his orderly. Asher had been eager to go from the moment he saw Nathan in uniform and learned that there was a possibility of getting into his company.

" And would I get to wear a uniform like that? " he asked.

" You'd not only get to," Nathan assured him; " you'd have to."

Young Samuel Rose wanted to go as badly as Asher, and Nathan admitted that Camp Winter Hill needed doctors more than any other kind of recruit. But Samuel and Elizabeth had a three-year-old son and were expecting another baby within the month. It would be unwise for Samuel to go at this time.

Shortly after Nathan returned from his furlough, Colonel Webb's regiment was ordered from Camp Winter Hill to Roxbury, a few miles away. The move made little difference, however, for life at Roxbury was very similar to the life at Winter Hill — so similar that Nathan and Hull agreed they would not have known they'd been moved except for the different angle of the sun's rays.

But at last, in March, the routine of the winter months was broken. Washington, according to what Nathan heard, was now ready to force the British to evacuate Boston. Colonel Webb's regiment, with other regiments stationed on the heights above the city, was ordered to loose a short cannonade each evening at sunset. One night two thousand men were ordered to start building fortifications on the heights. Nathan's and Hull's companies were among these. Soon the troops that had been stationed all winter at Winter Hill and Roxbury were reinforced by thousands of men. On March 17, Howe evacuated the city and Nathan felt that he had at last taken part in one small portion of the War for Independence.

Now that Boston was freed of the British, there was no longer reason for keeping fifteen thousand men at Roxbury and Winter Hill. Early in the spring of the fateful year of 1776, Washington began moving his Massachusetts and Connecticut troops to New York. Colonel Webb's regiment was the first to be called.

Plodding the muddy roads with his company as it marched to New London for the boat trip down the Sound, Nathan wondered if he would be able to see any of his friends in New London. But the soldiers boarded transports immediately, and all he saw of his friends was their hands waving from the crowd assembled at the docks.

The Union School boys were there in a body. Suddenly Nathan stared. Was that Eustacia? In New London? She was crying: " Nathan! Nathan! " Merriweather must have driven her clear over from East Haddam to see the troops off. Then he realized that the young man at her side was not dapper Trevor Merriweather, but a tall, homely fellow, angular and blond. Had Merriweather thought the call to arms more romantic than selling shoes? Or had Eustacia simply passed on to someone new again? Now that he had Alice back, he saw more clearly than ever what a mistake Eustacia would have been. But had it not been for her fickleness, he might have made the mistake. It seemed to him he had much to thank Eustacia for. He gave her a wave and a smile.

Nathan knew that Washington was bending every effort to fortify New York. After the evacuation of Boston, the British were sure to try to seize the city that was the principal seaport of the Atlantic coast as well as the main roadway to Canada.

His company, with the other companies of Colonel Webb's regiment, had plenty to do when they reached Long Island. The weather was fine, and the soldiers were in better spirits than they had been for a long time. The army was improving noticeably in discipline, and the fortifications went up rapidly.

True to expectations, British troops, under General Howe, landed on Staten Island, July 9.

That morning the sun beat down on the tents of Nathan's company with a heat that sapped the vitality of the men. He had determined not to do much drill, for it seemed to him that little was to be gained by

physical exertion in the torrid heat. But the order had
gone out for all companies to be on parade at eleven
o'clock.

When his company reached the parade grounds,
Nathan noticed that a speaker's stand had been erected.
He halted his men in the shade of a row of trees, the
perspiration dripping from his chin. Surely the weather
had never been so unbearable in Coventry. Soon orders
came to form in a hollow square about the speaker's
stand.

How much more like an army the men looked now,
he thought. " At ease " no longer meant slumping and
slouching. He turned his eyes from the soldiers toward
the speaker's stand, and felt his body tense. A cortege
was approaching on horseback, but he saw only the
central figure. Although he had seen the man on the
white horse only once before, there was no mistak-
ing him. He was General George Washington, Commander in Chief of the American Army. Absolute
stillness seemed to have fallen over the parade grounds.
Not a breath of wind stirred the grass.

General Washington dismounted and walked toward
the stand. On the platform he stood a moment in silence
before he spoke.

" Men of the Army of the United States of America,"
he began, " your Congress has adopted the following
Declaration of Independence, which it seems fitting and
proper that I should read to you at the earliest possible
moment." The firm, clear voice went on: " ' When in
the course of human events, it becomes necessary for
one people to dissolve the political bands which have

connected them with another, . . . a decent respect to the opinions of mankind requires that they should declare the causes which impel them to the separation.

" ' We hold these truths to be self-evident, that all men are created equal, that they are endowed by their Creator with certain unalienable Rights, that among these are Life, Liberty, and the pursuit of Happiness.' "

Nathan forgot the blistering sun.

" ' We, therefore, . . . solemnly publish and declare, That these United Colonies are, . . . Free and Independent States; that they are Absolved from all Allegiance to the British Crown, . . . and that as Free and Independent States, they have full Power to levy War, conclude Peace, contract Alliances, establish Commerce, and to do all other Acts and Things which Independent States may of right do. And for the support of this Declaration, with a firm reliance on the Protection of Divine Providence, we mutually pledge to each other our Lives, our Fortunes, and our sacred Honor.' "

The blood raced through Nathan's veins. Here was his dream come to reality. He did not doubt, now that the Colonies had declared their independence, that they would win the war and seal the declaration General Washington had read.

The exhilarating spirit of freedom seemed to touch his soul. All the rest of the day, words kept echoing in his ears. " Independence! " " Pursuit of Happiness! " " The United States of America! " " Liberty! " " Justice! " " Honor! " The one word that echoed oftener than any other was " Liberty."

CHAPTER 14

Personal Challenge

THE MAGNITUDE of the British preparations to attack New York grew, with each day bringing added reinforcements to the British ships anchored in the harbor. Soon, Nathan knew, the British would greatly outnumber the American forces stationed in the city. Yet all he could do was fret and watch the enemy pile up strength. The effect on his men was demoralizing. Food, clothing, and money were again cruelly short.

Nathan wondered how long this could go on. It took a long time to prepare for a landing from the sea, he knew. The longer the British took, the stronger their assault and the less able the American forces would be to meet the attack. He wished desperately that there was something he could do to allay his men's fears and to boost their morale.

One morning as he was anxiously scanning the activities in the harbor below, his glass caught something that had not been there the day before. Under the guns of a British man-of-war a sloop hovered like a lone chick under the wing of a large gray hen. He made out the name *Asia* on the side of the man-of-war. He peered intently through his spyglass, suddenly tense with excitement. Yes, he had been right. The newly arrived sloop was filled with provisions.

A daring idea came to him. If the sloop could be cut loose, how much that load of provisions would mean to the American troops!

As he started back to camp, the parts of a plan were falling into place in his mind. Only one point bothered him. The plan he had conceived should bear the sanction of Colonel Webb if it were to be executed, and yet he wondered. Webb was careful, conservative. Would he think it a wild scheme, too dangerous, too unlikely to succeed? Nathan was afraid so. If Webb refused his sanction, what then? Acting without orders was a court-martial offense. He did not want to act without orders. No one had worked harder than he to build up discipline in the raw troops that made up the American Army. Yet he felt that there was a higher law obligating him to see this through. If he went to Webb with the plan, he was desperately afraid it would die there.

By the time he had reached camp, he had made his decision. His step became quick and purposeful. He had to pick four men — the right four. That was the starting point.

That night he gathered the four around him in his tent.

" You understand," he said, " I'm doing this without orders. We could be court-martialed for it — every one of us. I don't want you to join me unless you are sure that you're willing to take the risk."

" I am, sir," spoke up a sandy-, curly-haired young

fellow named Smith whom Nathan had chosen because of his seamanship.

The other three without hesitation indicated their willingness.

"Not a word of this must leak out," Nathan warned them. "You understand? I hope you also understand why I'm doing this in the way I am. There are times when a man must be guided by what he feels in his own heart to be right, even though it violates some regulation. This is one of those times. I'll let you know the night for our job."

The supply ship remained under the wing of the *Asia*. Nathan felt reasonably sure its cargo was for use of the British Army after they were ashore, and that it would therefore remain undisturbed until he had time to bring his plan to action. He had set the mission for the following week. There would be no moon, and Smith would have a rowboat secreted in the brush on the shore of the East River.

As darkness approached on the fateful night, Nathan felt an almost overwhelming excitement and could not remain in his tent. He walked about the streets of the camp, impatient for darkness to fall. At ten o'clock he was to meet his men at the spot where the boat was hidden. Each would go alone to the rendezvous; each would follow a different route to reach it.

Finally, Nathan felt that it was dark enough to set out. He could hardly keep from breaking into a run as he cleared the outskirts of the camp. He felt in his pocket for the muffler that was so important a part of his plan. He wondered if the others had the equipment assigned to them — the ropes, the knives. He parted the bushes and reached out a hand to find the boat. A voice startled him.

" Captain? " came the faintest whisper. The whisperer was Smith.

When all five had reported, the boat was lifted on their shoulders, carried to the water's edge, and silently put down. Without haste, which might have occasioned some splashing of the oars, they rowed silently to a point opposite the *Asia* to wait till the darkest hour, just before dawn. The success of their enterprise, Nathan knew, would depend entirely on their ability to remain unseen and unsuspected until the moment for action arrived.

The night wore on, and there was no sound. Nathan found it increasingly difficult to wait patiently, and he knew this was also true of his companions. A fine rain began to fall, misting faces, dampening clothing, and chilling bodies. His limbs began to cramp.

At last he raised his arm, the prearranged signal, and the men rowed straight for the big ship. Nathan no longer felt the rain or the cold. Tense with excitement, he bent toward the looming shape which they were fast approaching.

The small boat drew close and the rowers rested on their oars. There was no sound, no movement from the deck of the vessel above them. Seconds stretched into minutes; then at last the watch passed, calling his " All's well! "

Nathan, his boots already off, scrambled up the side of the ship, hand over hand. He paused for a second, his eyes level with the deck. The watchman was only three feet away, his back turned. Nathan had the knitted muffler in his hand. Stealthily as a cat, he sprang. The muffler was over the watchman's mouth in an instant, and the man went down without a sound. Up went Nathan's free arm, the second signal. He felt rather than saw the others scrambling over the side. Silently they went to their tasks, Smith helping Nathan tie the arms and legs of the watchman, the others battening down the hatches over the sleeping crew. And still there was no sound.

They cut the sloop loose from the *Asia* and headed her for shore. Nathan took the tiller and felt the pounding of his heart. Surely at any moment the *Asia's* big guns would boom out; but if they did, he was determined to escape with his prize. They slipped away from the dim, looming shape; the chick was now out from under the shelter of its mother's wing. The distance widened. Still no shot boomed forth. It seemed unbelievable to Nathan that they could be moving steadily for shore, with the lights of the *Asia* growing dim in the distance. It was fantastic!

Dawn was just breaking when the sloop slid smoothly up along a wharf. News of its arrival spread wildly as the oddly assorted men on the pier who had seen her come in ran through the streets crying out the tidings. By the time the sloop had been made fast, the whole town seemed to have descended upon her.

" Sounds like a flock of sea gulls," Nathan said to the other four, a great relief in his heart. An instant later he saw Colonel Webb approaching. He stepped out of the boat, came to attention, and saluted.

" I will expect you at headquarters in ten minutes," Webb said sternly. " How many were with you? "

" Four, sir."

" Bring them."

" Yes, sir."

The elation Nathan had felt over the success of the enterprise was dimmed by anxiety, yet underneath was the deep satisfaction of knowing that now the troops would be fed.

" Well, here we go," he said, motioning to his companions. A few minutes later they stood before Colonel Webb.

" This was your plan, I presume, Captain Hale? " Webb asked.

" Yes, sir."

" It was, of course, a flagrant violation of military discipline for which I thought you had the highest respect. Will you please explain your actions? "

Nathan gave his story. Without waste of words he told his superior officer, as he had told his picked men, why he thought the good they could do the cause justified their action.

When he had finished speaking, Webb sat looking at his desk. Presently the Colonel raised his head and looked at the men who stood with Nathan before him.

" You felt as your captain did? " he asked them.

" We went with him, sir," young Smith said, standing proud and erect.

Webb turned his eyes to Nathan. " You will make an official report," he said, " as soon as possible. But first, go over the ship with the quartermaster, prepare an inventory, and be ready to unload by noon. You are dismissed."

So that was all! There was to be no punishment. An " official report " would make their action " regular." Nathan smiled at the four who had followed him as they left the headquarters tent.

By noon the work of loading the provisions onto wagons was well under way. Nathan stepped out on the deck of the sloop, his arm over the shoulder of Hull, who had come down to congratulate him. He was laughing, his light-brown hair blown back from his high forehead by the wind. A cheer went up from the crowd. He waved his hand.

Hull tapped his shoulder and nodded toward an approaching messenger. The orderly came to attention and saluted.

" A message for you from General Washington, Captain Hale."

Nathan took the message, opened it, and read:

Captain Hale:

This is to commend you for the courage and ability displayed in the execution of your carefully wrought plan for obtaining provisions for the United States Army from the British man-of-war *Asia,* and to request that you report to me personally.

By order of:

George Washington,
Commander in Chief of the United States Army.

" I'm to tell you, sir," the messenger added, " to report to Colonel Knowlton, who will conduct you to General Washington."

" It's true, Hull! " Nathan cried. " I'm not dreaming." Never before had he known the thrill that swept through him. " As soon as I finish — " His one thought now was to hurry the unloading.

When the task was completed, he reported to Colonel Knowlton. Washington's headquarters was a fine old estate a few miles out of New York at Murray Hill. A colored servant received them in a wide, circular hall dominated by a fine crystal chandelier. Underfoot the carpeting was thick and soft. Nathan could not help contrasting the richness of carpeting and chandelier with the Spartan simplicity of a tent.

" Colonel Knowlton and Captain Hale," the servant announced.

They passed from the hall into a long, paneled room, cool and comfortable on this August day. The Commander in Chief sat at the far end behind a desk. Nathan thought, as he crossed the room, how well he had remembered everything about Washington — the tone of his voice, the expression of his eyes, the words he had spoken at The Happy Warrior. Would Washington remember him?

" General Washington, Captain Nathan Hale."

Nathan thought he caught a quizzical look in the General's keen gray eyes as he acknowledged Knowlton's introduction. " You did a fine thing for the United States' cause this morning, Captain Hale."

It was the same sincere, deep voice. The only change

three years had wrought, Nathan thought, was a deep-
ening of dignity, an increasing seriousness, an older
look. Older? His mind questioned the word. Not older
— greater — as though the Commander in Chief had
grown with his responsibilities.

" I wondered, Captain Hale, when I heard of your
feat, if you realized the importance of what you had
done. I see that you do. We have at no time since the
conflict began needed an efficient and loyal army as
badly as now. What you did will greatly help the morale
of the troops. I wish to express my appreciation to you
personally and to ask that you also convey my appreciation to those who accompanied you."

" Thank you, sir." Nathan's heart swelled.

" You will pardon my asking," Washington said suddenly, " but I wonder if we have not met before."

" We sat at the same table, sir, nearly three years ago
at The Happy Warrior, on the post road near Boston."

For a moment Nathan was disappointed. The slightly
puzzled look that had come into Washington's eyes did
not alter. Then he saw that the General had remembered. A smile came into the serious eyes and played
over the stern lips.

" I remember now. You are the young man from
Yale."

" Yes, sir. We talked together about the plight of the
Colonies."

" Yes, indeed. I remember thinking that evening that
it was men like you that the Colonies needed."

" You said as much, sir." Nathan's voice was unsteady with emotion. "I have never forgotten your words."

For a moment Washington did not speak. Then, "May my judgment be as good in all the affairs that are now in my hands," the General said.

CHAPTER 15

Discouraging Days

COLONEL WEBB's regiment, stationed on a hill at the rear, did not get into the thick of the disastrous Battle of Long Island. From that hill, which flanked the rear, Nathan saw the day's desperation. The American cause, depleted in strength, seemed hopeless. An epidemic of fever had broken out during August, and General Greene, with many of his men, lay prostrate.

Nathan helplessly watched the slaughter. Bayonets stabbed and muskets were wielded as clubs. In the lower harbor the guns of the British fleet roared. The disintegrating American troops were attacked on three sides, and those who turned to run found no place to go but into the treacherous bogs.

At twilight, General Howe called off his troops, and the Americans began the almost hopeless task of trying to bring order out of chaos. All night long rain fell, drenching the ill and the wounded. The rain continued and fighting was desultory the second day. General Sullivan and General Stirling had been taken prisoners. Surrender seemed inevitable unless the American troops could be removed without the knowledge of the

British, for they would be cut off by the fleet if they were discovered attempting to retreat across the water from Long Island to New York.

But the weather, which had seemed to be against the hard-pressed Americans, was with them in the end. By nightfall of August 29, the rain turned to a heavy fog. Under cover of this blinding curtain, Washington skillfully withdrew his maimed and depleted troops, removing them by small boats. Morning found Long Island in the hands of the British, but it was an empty Long Island. No American soldier was left on the island.

Safe in New York, Nathan went from tent to tent trying to cheer ill and dispirited men. It was hard to do anything for their morale now. They had accepted defeat. This one battle seemed to be the war, and they had lost it. Everything was over. They might as well go home, which all too many of them were doing.

"We've simply lost one battle," Nathan told a disconsolate group of men sitting cold and miserable about their campfire. September had come in damp and chill. " It's our first loss of consequence. We can't give up the first time things go against us. If everybody deserted and went home, what good would be our Declaration of Independence? We'd be England's again, and in for such punishment as I hate to think of."

But Nathan's encouraging voice soon faltered, for the fever that had attacked so many now attacked him. He went into his tent one afternoon from making the rounds of the sick and threw himself on his cot. Today his spirit was heavy. What could Washington hope to do, he wondered, with men deserting by the hundreds and with those who remained already defeated in their minds? Sooner or later the British would attack New York itself. What could this disorganized, demoralized, straggling army hope to do against a well-disciplined, expertly trained force of twenty-five thousand men?

An hour later Asher Wright came into the tent.

" Captain," he said.

Nathan moved restlessly, but did not speak. He felt Asher touch his head. And then Asher was struggling with clumsy fingers to remove his wet boots.

" What are you doing? " Nathan asked, half opening his eyes.

" Taking off your boots. You'll catch cold lying there."

" I'm not going to lie here." Nathan sat up, his hand to his head.

" Head ache? " Asher asked.

" Sort of."

" Lie down," Asher said, throwing a blanket over him and pushing him back upon the cot.

" It's not bedtime," Nathan demurred vaguely.

" Stay right there," Asher said, " I'm going for the Doc. You're ill." He was no longer Captain Hale's orderly; he was Nathan Hale's friend. He had loved him since the Coventry days when they were both young boys.

Nathan lay still, his hand over his eyes. Little knives of pain pierced his eyeballs and stabbed into his head. He dozed again and did not know that Asher had returned to the tent with a doctor. Nor was he conscious of the doctor's orders to have him removed to the hospital.

" No," Asher protested. " I promised his folks I'd take care of him. Now when he needs me I'm not going to be put off. You're too crowded in the hospitals, and you haven't enough nurses. Let him stay here; I'll nurse him. I'll carry out your orders. I used to help Doc Rose at home."

Through the long days and nights that followed, Nathan tossed in delirium and grew steadily weaker.

" If only I could get Doc Rose here," Asher said aloud one day as he stood helplessly by the cot.

Through his delirium, Nathan caught the name.

" Doc, Doc," he said fretfully, " look after Alice. I promised her."

Asher despaired. He was following the camp doctor's orders to the letter, but Nathan was no better. He stepped outside the tent to get away, for a moment, from the sound of his friend's labored breathing.

" O Asher! "

He looked up to see young Jonathan Means coming toward the tent. Jonathan was one of the eleven recruits who had come back with Nathan when he returned from Coventry.

" How's Captain Hale? " Jonathan asked.

Asher's eyes were heavy. " Bad."

Jonathan said: " I've got leave. I'm starting for Coventry in the morning. What shall I tell his folks? "

Asher's face lighted. " I've been wishing I could get word to Doc Rose. If he'd come, maybe everything would be all right."

"You want Doc Rose to come to New York?" Jonathan asked.

"If you tell him how bad Nathan is, he'll come."

For eight months Asher had carefully said "Captain Hale." He did not realize that this time he had used the name "Nathan."

The black days and nights went on. Nathan's voice, in delirium, grew weaker, and the veins stood out on his thin hands. One morning, Asher stumbled out of the tent after a sleepless night, his hair tousled and his eyes glazed. It seemed that a voice had called his name. Two men were coming toward him and one was a soldier. With the soldier was a civilian whose walk seemed familiar.

"Asher, old man," a voice called, "how's Nathan?"

"Doc Rose!" Asher cried out. "Thank heaven you're here!"

They went together into the tent. The doctor bent over Nathan.

A low incessant mumbling came from the cot. "The provisions. The troops must have provisions."

The doctor shook his head.

"Don't *you* do that," Asher pleaded. "That's all the other doctors do."

Doc Rose straightened up. "I've brought someone with me who can probably do more than I can — if we can get her through. Alice came down with me. Nothing would keep her from coming. I told her I wouldn't be able to get her into camp, but she came."

"You mean Alice is here?" Asher's fogged brain groped. "In New York?"

"Yes. They wouldn't let her come into camp with me, but I promised to see if anything could be done. Whom can we see?"

"She's here, and they wouldn't let her come to Nathan?" Asher's blurred eyes had cleared. "Where is she? I'll get her in."

Nathan fretted in delirium. "Don't argue with pa, Doc. It's no good. Don't argue —"

Doc Rose took Asher's arm, and they went outside. "Who would have some influence?" the doctor asked. "If we can wangle permission somehow —"

"Captain Hull!" Asher said suddenly. "He's Nathan's best friend. He's been to see him every day. He'll go to Colonel Webb for us. He'll even go to Washington if he has to. The General's Nathan's friend." Asher was off on a run.

The doctor stepped back inside the tent.

The restless voice muttered incessantly. "Let me alone, Asher. Don't take my boots off. I'm going to get up."

"Lie still," Doc Rose said soothingly. "Here, swallow this. Alice will be here soon."

Alice! Alice! Nathan's fever-hazed brain wandered off to a grassy nook at the end of a lane where he waited for Alice to jump down over the bank to him. He turned fitfully on the pillow.

"Why doesn't she come? Why is she late?"

A shadow moved at the tent's opening. A figure came and went swiftly to the cot.

"I'm here, Nathan," Alice said, breathless.

The fevered eyes widened. "You mustn't stay long.

You'll get cold. Just be brave, Alice — " Words dwindled off, and Nathan slept, holding Alice's hand.

She looked up at Doc Rose searchingly.

" We'll do our best," he told her.

Asher threw himself on his own cot and was asleep at once.

Days and nights of endless waiting and watching followed. Then one morning just as the light of day began to vie with the light of the candle in the tent, Nathan said, clearly and distinctly, " Alice, where are you? "

She was on her feet in an instant and at Nathan's side. Doc Rose nodded and smiled.

" Alice, you're really here? "

" Yes, Nathan, I'm really here."

Nathan sighed a long sigh that held contentment.

Doc Rose motioned to Asher, and they went out. The crisis was past.

CHAPTER 16

Valiant Volunteer

IN THE early autumn twilight Colonel Knowlton walked with bowed head toward the officers' tent. He had just come from General Washington's headquarters, and his heart was heavy. His commander had given him a most difficult order, and tonight he must carry it out.

Knowlton had found Washington himself discouraged and anxious. Talking frankly, the commander had painted a dismal picture. His men were now deserting in companies. Those that were left were ill and underfed, discouraged, unpaid, and nearly a third of them actually without shelter, with another winter coming on. If he knew where the British were going to strike, then, despite his army's pitiful condition, he might be able to pull it together to fight. But since he was in blind ignorance of where the attack would come, the situation looked hopeless. Perhaps the British planned to hem in the town; perhaps they intended to cut the Army off from the states. He could think of all kinds of things they *might* do, but the point was to find out what they were planning. The fate of the American

Army, probably the fate of the whole cause of independence, lay in that knowledge.

Knowlton, looking grave, had agreed. But he had looked more than grave at Washington's next words.

" Colonel Knowlton, I must have intelligence of the enemy's plans. I have chosen you to get it for me. I want you to call together a group of officers — I am trusting their choice to you — officers of superior loyalty, intelligence, integrity. From that group, I want you to find a man who will go into the British lines and obtain the intelligence I must have."

" I will do what I can," Knowlton had said gravely. " But that will be spying, and officers, sir — "

" Nevertheless, I must have an educated man, one with a knowledge of draftsmanship. One who can discover the enemy's plans and reproduce them. Haste is imperative. Find me a man no later than tomorrow."

Knowlton had picked his men and had sent word to them to meet him here at seven. In less than a half hour he must ask a difficult thing of them. Anything in the accepted line of honorable duty he would have felt no hesitancy in asking. But spying! The very word smelled of dishonor, and calling it another name made it no more palatable. He turned away from the officers' tent and circled back, trying to walk off his dread and sustain his courage. He would a thousand times rather lead his men into battle than face the little group he had summoned. He looked at his watch and found he could delay no longer. He walked quickly toward the tent.

The men he had summoned looked at him questioningly as he stepped in front of them. He straightened to his full stature and, by a conscious effort, held his chin high.

" Men," he said, " I have come from General Washington's headquarters. He commissioned me to lay a message before you. General Washington feels it imperative to obtain information in regard to the enemy's movements and plans with reference to the attack on New York. He desired me to call you together and explain to you the grim situation. Without knowledge of the enemy's expectations, he fears a recurrence of the Long Island disaster. He feels that the fate of our cause lies in discovering the plans of the British. He needs definite information as to where and when they plan to attack. He has put a great responsibility on my shoulders, and yours, in asking that such information be obtained. But this is not a task that he wishes to impose by command. He asks that someone volunteer for the service."

There was silence in the tent. Then Captain Maynard rose to his feet. He was a tall, dark-eyed man, one of the most respected and best-liked of the officers.

" Colonel Knowlton, sir," he said, " is this spying you're asking us to do? "

Knowlton bit his lip but did not reply.

Someone else spoke up, " Is this something honorable you're asking us to do? "

" Isn't it honorable to serve your country? " Knowlton defended.

There was a general hubbub of disapproving voices.

" But the means, sir — "

" After all, we're officers."

" The disgrace, sir — "

Knowlton was torn between sympathy and understanding, and the urgency of the need with which Washington had commissioned him. He wet his lips.

" Gentlemen! " he said. Silence fell, and he wondered how to go on. " We are in desperate circumstances — "

Someone raised the tent flap and slipped in quietly. Colonel Knowlton paused for a moment. The late arrival was Nathan, still pale and thin from his recent illness. Colonel Knowlton waited until the others had moved and made room.

" I would be the last man to ask such a sacrifice of you," he went on, " if I did not feel, with General Washington, that we must get intelligence of the British intentions at once."

" You're asking us to go into the British lines? " a voice asked.

" How else can we get the information? " Colonel Knowlton snapped, his nerves straining.

" Isn't that too much to ask of any officer? " another voice condemned. " A man would carry infamy with his name the rest of his days. He would be scorned by his own men."

A quiet voice, not very strong, but very clear, said, " I will undertake the mission, sir."

The silence that followed the words was breathless. Then the officers were on their feet.

" You can't do that. Hale."

" Think what it could mean."

" What if you should be captured? "

Captain Hull made his way to Nathan's side. " No, Nathan! You haven't thought what you're saying. You would have to go in disguise. It's spying."

But Nathan only smiled at his old friend.

Colonel Knowlton's face was white. To what was he sending this boy?

" Where and when do I report, Colonel? " Nathan asked.

" I wonder if you're physically able? " Colonel Knowlton sought escape.

" I'm quite all right now, sir."

The Colonel sighed. " Then you will report to General Washington at the first possible moment tomorrow morning at Murray Hill."

" Yes, sir."

Nathan turned toward the door. He wanted to get out, away from the others, to be alone. He did not know that Hull started to follow him, thought better of it, and turned into the tent. He did not see the look of accusation Hull gave Colonel Knowlton. He did not hear Knowlton's voice saying:

" I know. I know."

Outside the tent, Nathan whispered to himself: " Alice, Alice, be with me again as you were a little while ago when I was ill. God, give me strength — "

He hardly knew whether he was praying, or whether his soul was communing with Alice as he went back through the September night to his tent. The stars were out, and he looked up at them. They had always seemed so close to him, ever since he was a little boy. And Alice loved them too.

" You won't think it dishonorable, will you, Alice? You'll understand? "

He straightened his shoulders and went into his tent and found Asher idly rolling a pair of dice on the floor.

" That's against orders, Asher! Get out my trunk and get me the homespun suit I wore before I put on uniform. Get out my Yale diploma, and a couple of books, and my schoolbag."

Asher pulled the little trunk into the middle of the floor. Nathan lay on his cot and watched. He had not yet got his strength back entirely, and the excitement of his decision had tired him.

Hull raised the tent flap.

" Come in, Captain." Nathan raised himself on his elbow.

Hull glanced at the diploma in Asher's hand. " Nathan, you can't do it, you with your honesty. Think of your future."

Nathan reached for Hull's hand. " Please don't think me foolish, but I feel — I feel as if I'd been called to do this, as if it were the purpose I was put here for. I've never done anything that was worth much in the world, and I've always longed to do something worthy."

" What about Alice? "

Nathan did not answer for a moment. Asher had quit his work and was sitting on his haunches by the little trunk.

" She'll understand," Nathan said.

"But think how it's going to hurt her. The disgrace of spying —" Hull knew he was scraping a knife across his friend's heart.

Nathan stood up. "I would give my life to save her from being hurt, but I can't deny this call. I must report to Washington in the morning."

Hull went out, and Nathan was conscious of Asher's unhappy eyes.

"Wrap those things in a bundle, Asher," he said. "My set of drawing tools and some foolscap too. I'll take them with me in the morning."

Asher obeyed.

"And Asher," Nathan hesitated a moment, "if anything should happen that I — don't get back — see that the little trunk goes home. My commission and all my papers are in it. My camp book's there too, and there's a diary. Silly, isn't it, keeping a diary?" He laughed, but without humor. "Well, I'd like Alice to have those if anything should happen."

"Yes, Captain," Asher said over a lump in his throat.

As he lay awake on his cot that night, Nathan thought out the details. He would have to take someone with him in the morning to bring back his horse in case Washington wanted him to go direct from Murray Hill. He had decided to go as a schoolmaster; if the schoolmaster disguise met with Washington's approval, everything was ready. It seemed to him that the most convincing role he could play would be that of a schoolmaster of Tory sympathies seeking a position, for he had been a teacher long enough for the role to come naturally. He only prayed he could get the information Washington wanted.

He was up the next morning before the men were stirring. He had decided to take Asher along to Murray Hill. He would have liked to have Hull, but Asher had been faithful and would not remonstrate with him. Then, just as they were mounting, Hull was suddenly at his side, holding out his hand.

Nathan gripped it hard. " Don't think harshly of me, Hull."

" I think God never made a nobler man. Good-by, and God be with you, Hale Secundus."

The old college nickname was poignant. " Good-by, Hull." Nathan spurred his horse.

It was still early when he arrived at Murray Hill, so he was undecided whether or not he should present himself immediately. Perhaps Washington would be at breakfast, or not yet up. He pondered for a moment, looking at the fine old white house that had been built, he had been told, by a wealthy Quaker. No, he decided, he would not delay; Washington had stressed the need of haste. He dismounted and went up the broad steps. The door was opened by the same Negro who had admitted him following the capture of the sloop. Odd, he thought, that Knowlton had brought him the first time, and Knowlton had sent him the second time. Or had it been Knowlton's sending? Perhaps he had sent himself.

" Captain Nathan Hale," he said to the Negro. " Tell General Washington that Colonel Knowlton sent me."

" Yas, suh."

He walked restlessly about the reception hall, looking

at the fine wood paneling and the chandelier. Soon the
Negro was back.

" De Gen'ral will see you now, suh."

Would he be ushered into the dining room, or into
some private sitting room? But the Negro was leading
him toward the familiar door that led into the long,
cool room with the high, beamed ceiling. General
Washington was at his desk at the far end of the room.
It seemed a long walk down the dim corridor of the
room, but at last he stood before his commander.

" So it's you, Captain Hale," Washington said, looking at him intently. " Won't you sit down? " He
motioned to a chair on the other side of the desk.
" Colonel Knowlton sent you? You understand the
mission? "

" Yes, sir."

" You volunteered? "

" Yes, sir."

For a moment Washington did not speak. Presently
he sighed and shifted his position. " It is imperative
that we have accurate intelligence of the intended
moves of the enemy in and about New York. There is
no way to obtain such information, I am sorry to say,
except by crossing into the British lines in disguise. You
are aware, I am sure, that such a course involves serious
risk. May I commend you, for the second time, Captain
Hale, on your courage."

" Thank you, sir."

" It is a high sense of duty that sends you on such a
mission." Then General Washington changed his tone
and became terse. " I will give you a general order to

any owner of an American craft in Long Island Sound to convey you to any point on Long Island. You will go to Norwalk before attempting to cross because of the danger from the small British cruisers in the waters off nearer points. Have you thought of a disguise? "

" I had thought of going as a schoolmaster, as I have my diploma, and my schoolbag and some books. I could wear the brown homespun that I wore when teaching and would feel very much at home. I brought the things with me."

Washington nodded. " You can reach Norwalk by evening and cross the Sound under cover of darkness."

" Yes, sir."

Washington began to spread out maps on the desk, and Nathan's heartbeat quickened.

" The enemy are camped here — and here — and here — "

Nathan followed the explanations intently. Every position pointed out to him seemed to flash an immediate and accurate picture to his brain. All of his senses were acute, as though sharpened by this unusual necessity.

" Yes, sir," he nodded, " yes, sir," as the tense, serious voice went on with the explanations and instructions.

Washington straightened from his maps.

" Your command of Latin is, of course, good, and you are an able draftsman? "

" Yes, sir."

" Then you will take all notes in Latin. Draw your plans accurately. Here is paper of minute thickness. It will be more readily concealed."

The instructions were completed. General Washington rose and extended his hand.

" If there were more men like you in the American Army," he said, " I would have no fears. God bless you."

CHAPTER 17

Betrayal

NATHAN HAD Asher Wright for company on the ride to Norwalk. There he changed from regimentals to homespun, and boarded the little junk that would carry him across the Sound. His instructions to his boyhood friend were explicit. In five days Asher was to come back, cross to the Long Island shore before daylight, and pick him up. These instructions given, he said good-by.

Two hours before dawn the junk deposited him on Long Island.

" There's an inn a half mile or so up the road," the boatman said, " kept by the Widow Chichester. Likely ye kin git a bed there."

Nathan had no intention of going to the Widow Chichester's, at least not before he had established his character in the neighborhood. He knew the inn well. It was a popular gathering place for Tories, and the widow was a keen one who had an eye peeled for likely-looking prospects for the British ranks. She might prove valuable later on, but not now when his early-morning arrival might arouse suspicion. He wouldn't want to try out on the widow his story of being a Dutch schoolmaster with Tory sympathies. He would try it first on some less keen, less suspecting persons.

He walked down the road past the inn, and went on a couple of miles. Daylight spread across the land. Not wanting to arouse suspicion by walking the roads at dawn, he climbed a fence into a pasture at the roadside and waited. When the sun was well up, he approached a farmhouse and asked for breakfast. Here he would initiate his story.

It was a pleasant-looking place, and a placid-faced woman was busy about the kitchen. She accepted his story without question, fed him well, thanked him heartily for the money he gave her for his breakfast, and wished him well in obtaining work. The success of his story at its first telling increased his confidence amazingly. He whistled as he plodded up the road. This was a desperate, life-and-death game, but if he were clever enough he could win.

The developments of the next three days increased his confidence. People accepted his story and made friends with him. Gradually he made his way through each of the British camps, his keen mind taking in every detail, his ears alert for any word about the attack on New York. It wasn't hard to get the soldiers to talk, but it was from the young officers, in the evening, that he secured the most accurate information. Late each night he worked over his notes and drawings. He was getting what Washington wanted, and he should be through at the appointed time. If he didn't make it back in five days, he would make it in six, and Asher would wait for him. If this could turn the tide for the

American forces, he could feel he had lived up to the
challenge Washington had given him: " It's men like
you that will lift the yoke of British tyranny."

Often his thoughts went to Alice. How wonderful it
had been of her to come to him when he was ill! Would
he be here now, he wondered, had it not been for her?
Washington should know how a black-haired girl had
played a part in this expedition! With sudden impatience, he wished the war was over. He and Alice had
lost too much time.

The night of September 20, Nathan worked fever-
ishly. He believed he had everything he needed. He
drew the last plan of the fortifications, wrote, in Latin,
the last detail of the intended campaign. Tomorrow he
would reach the shore at dawn. Asher would have found
a boat and would be patrolling the Sound. He shouldn't
be noticed at such an early hour.

All that remained was to fold the last of the thin
papers carefully and place them between the soles of
his shoes with the papers already there. He had bought
a pair of insoles in Norwalk, and although they made
the fit of his boots a trifle snug, they had served the
purpose well.

He put on his boots and slung his schoolbag over his
shoulder. Three miles to go, then an American boat and
Asher, then his horse, then the fifty miles back to Murray Hill and Washington!

He slipped quietly down the stairs and let himself
out of the back door of the farmhouse at which he had
paid for a bed for the night. The road was dark; the
tang of early fall was in the air. As he came up with the

lights of the Widow Chichester's Inn, a group of young British officers stumbled unsteadily down the steps. They were far from sober after a night of merrymaking. Nathan recognized them. He had been with them frequently during the past few days, but he hoped they would not recognize him now, for he wanted no delay.

This hope was doomed to disappointment.

" Aha, it's our clever schoolmaster! " one cried.

" What brings you out on the road this time of night? " called another.

" This time of night? " Nathan bantered. " Why, you devils you, don't you know it's morning, and time for a man to get his breakfast? "

" Why, man, it's as dark as midnight! "

" It's cloudy, that's all, and you're foggy. How many quarts did you stow away? "

" Not enough. Come along, and we'll find some more."

" No, thanks; I'm bent on getting my breakfast."

There was nothing to do after that but turn in to the Widow Chichester's. Nathan, who had been accepted there as a friend of the British officers, didn't mind going into the inn, but he chafed at the waste of time. However, there was nothing else for it, so he might as well have a cup of coffee and a bite of food.

He sat at a little table with his back to the door, and ordered bacon and eggs. He was hungry, and the food was good. There were a number of men about the room, some stretched out on the benches, others busying themselves with food. It was a place where all kinds of people came for all kinds of reasons, Nathan ruminated. He ate rapidly, for a faint streak of light was showing through the east window. He still had half a mile to go. He swallowed his last bite whole and pushed back his chair.

As he turned toward the door, he caught sight of a dark, strangely familiar head. For a minute he couldn't think where he had seen that head; then, as the man left, he noticed the arrogant lift of the broad shoulders and he knew. It was either his cousin Sam Hale or someone very much like him. Sam probably *would* be in Tory territory, for he had always had strong Tory leanings.

Nathan left the inn quickly, anxious not to draw the attention of this man who might be Sam Hale. The early-morning light was still dim when he reached the shore. Although the sun was up, the day actually was cloudy, as he had told the young officers. He strained his eyes and saw a scow approaching rapidly.

From that distance, he wondered, could Asher see him on the shore? The boat seemed to be aiming for a point above him. He raised his arm in signal, but the boat did not change its course. It was probably too dark for him to be seen.

" Asher! " he called. " Asher! "

He ran along the shore, calling and motioning, and the boat turned toward him. He could have whooped as he and Enoch and John had done when they were little tads. In a few minutes now he would be back in the American lines, and he had what he had gone after.

The boat came poling in. He stepped to the water's

edge. Two men jumped out, caught him, and pinioned his arms. Neither was Asher!

" Where are you going? " Nathan asked. His heart was pounding with terrific force.

" What difference does that make? "

" I was trying to find someone to help me. I'm a deserter from the rebel's ranks, and I want to join the regulars."

Just then a crouching form arose from the bushes a few rods up the shore. The man straightened and seemed to nod at the men in the boat. As though they had been given a signal, they thrust their captive forward and pushed him into the boat.

Nathan's breath caught in his throat. Again he had seen broad shoulders that moved with an arrogant lift. His cousin Sam had recognized him at the inn and had brought about his capture.

CHAPTER 18

Destiny Fulfilled

THE CAPTORS were silent at the oars, and Nathan's thoughts raced desperately on plans for escape. But beneath his fear ran an undercurrent of bitterness. To be betrayed by your own kin was hard. How much had the Eustacia affair had to do with it? He saw again the black anger of fallen pride on Sam's face the night Eustacia had told him of her engagement. But his Tory sympathies had been strong too. At any rate, regardless of the reason, Sam had betrayed him. He could jump from the boat and swim for shore, but if the rowers did not overtake him, certainly Sam would be waiting when he reached land. Probably it was best to wait, trusting to the blind future.

He hadn't long to wait. The boat rounded a bend, and a British man-of-war, hidden behind a wooded point, loomed into sight. Steadily the oarsmen pulled toward it.

Nathan found himself delivered to a Captain Quarme. Outwardly at ease he repeated the story he had told his captors. He was relieved to see that Captain Quarme believed him.

"We'll take you up to General Howe tonight,"

Quarme said. " That's orders — all rebel deserters to headquarters. Howe'll fix you up."

Nathan's relief was gone; a chill ran down his spine. " He'll fix you up! " If no means of escape offered itself before then — Courage! Courage!

The long day wore on. Would they find the papers if they searched him at headquarters? What was poor Asher thinking as the hours went by and he did not return? In some way the papers concealed in his shoes must get through to Washington.

His heart was heavy as the *Halifax* docked at Turtle Bay at sunset, and its friendly young captain sent him on his way under armed guard. All day long he had believed that some means of escape would present itself. He was on the side of right, and right would prevail. But as he was marched to the mansion at Mount Pleasant where General Howe had his headquarters, his confidence sagged. Twilight settled about him. This was the hour he had expected to be approaching the familiar white mansion on Murray Hill. Instead, he was nearing the headquarters of the enemy's high command. His heart ached with despair.

He scarcely saw the wide lawns, with their prim borders, or the few patches of color left in the formal gardens. He had expected to be shown immediately to General Howe, and was surprised when he was turned over to the officer of the day, a handsome, well-set-up fellow of about forty whose name was Montressor. But of course! This was merely a routine matter; deserters were brought in every day. He was no different from any other deserter. Perhaps there was still a chance. If they didn't discover the papers, he would find a way out.

A Sergeant North took him by the arm.

" Proceed, Sergeant," Montressor ordered, and stood quietly at one side.

Sergeant North began a routine search. He un- buckled Nathan's belt. " Take off your boots," he com- manded.

Nathan's fingers were cold, but he knew he must dis- play no nervousness. This was the crucial moment. There was still a chance. If only they didn't find the inner soles! They fit well; he had made sure of that at the outset. He pulled off one boot and dropped it to the floor. The noise it made sounded in the room like a shot.

The sergeant reached for the boot, and Nathan bent to remove the other one. Don't watch the sergeant! Don't act nervous! Go right on with the boot as if nothing were happening! He didn't raise his eyes from what he was doing, yet he could see the sergeant turn the boot over and look at the bottom as if to determine how many miles it had tramped and then run his finger- nail along the seam to see if the stitching had been ripped.

Nathan tugged at the other boot. He dropped it on the floor and glanced at Montressor. Montressor's eyes were following the sergeant's movements intently as the man ran his hand down inside the boot he held. There was no sound in the room, unless it was the beat- ing of Nathan's heart. It sounded as loud in his ears as the beating of drums.

Into the quiet, the captain spoke three words. " Your knife, Sergeant."

They fell like a death knell on Nathan's ears. He could not even pray. In fascination his eyes moved to the sergeant. He had opened his knife and was running it down into the boot. Now he was prying with the point. By the sudden set of his lips, Nathan knew what he had found.

Captain Montressor stepped to the sergeant's side, and Nathan's head dropped for an instant in despair. Then he took a long breath, set his lips, raised his head, and squared his shoulders. Captain Montressor and the sergeant pried the insole out and removed the neatly folded sheets of thin paper with their carefully written words and their carefully drawn plans.

Captain Montressor looked at Nathan. " I didn't think you looked like an ordinary rebel deserter," he said.

Suddenly Nathan realized that the British officer's eyes were sorrowful.

" The other boot," Montressor said to the sergeant and tossed the one from which the insole had been removed to Nathan. " Get it on."

Nathan obeyed with numb fingers. One boot on, then the other. He wasn't thinking; he could only feel. His whole heart cried out to Alice. He stood between two guards that had come at Montressor's call. His body dragged, carrying a heavy load of failure and despair. Yet he made himself walk like a soldier as he followed the captain, who carried the sheets of paper spread out in his hand like a fan.

The door opened on a room of startling beauty, dominated by a white fireplace bordered with lovely delft-blue tiles, like a delicate gem exquisitely set. But Nathan's eyes, usually so quick to see beauty, saw only the man who sat behind a large mahogany desk. He might have been General Washington. He had the same military bearing, the same white-powdered wig.

Captain Montressor handed Howe the paper. There was now only one way it could end.

General Howe examined the sheets and looked up. " Drawings of our groundworks and fortifications. And notes in Latin. This can mean, of course, but one thing."

" Yes, sir," Nathan replied. It was the first word he had spoken, and his voice sounded far away to him and as if it came from another person.

" Do you have anything to say for yourself? " General Howe's words were clipped.

" Nothing except what you can see. I was inside your lines to obtain information."

" You are not in uniform."

" No, sir."

" What is your rank? "

" Captain."

" Your name?

" Hale. Nathan Hale."

The general turned back to the papers before him. There was no sound in the room but the light crackling of the thin sheets as he turned them. The minutes ticked away. Nathan tried to swallow but found it difficult. The general continued to study the notes.

" Captain Hale," he said finally, " I've never seen so excellent a set of drawings or so complete a set of notes." He looked intently at the young man standing straight and tall before him, and continued: " We could use such a man as you, if you would be interested in joining the British ranks. We would make it well worth your while, both in salary and in position."

Suddenly Nathan became taller. " Nothing," he said, " could make me turn traitor to my country! "

" You leave me but one course, Captain Hale."

" Yes, sir."

" It is my unpleasant duty to sentence you to be hanged as a spy tomorrow morning at sunrise. God be with you. That will be all, Captain Montressor." Howe's fingers shook as he gathered up the thin, neatly covered sheets of paper that lay on his desk.

" Take Captain Hale to the provost marshal and acquaint him with General Howe's orders," Montressor snapped at the guard.

Nathan scarcely saw the provost marshal to whom he was delivered. Suddenly a loud, rough voice snarled at him:

" Another di   n low-livered son-o

" I beg your p   ever, in his twenty-one years had he been so addressed. Startled from his numbness, he saw a short, fat, coarse-featured, red-faced man with an animal brutality in his eyes and on his curling lips. In his ugly fat hand the man held a blacksnake, which he twitched menacingly against his boot.

1993

He must be around sixty years of age, Nathan thought, and he must have spent those years viciously, to have a face so deeply engraved with lines of brutality.

He had gone so far in his thoughts when a sudden, sharp pain cut across his limbs. The man had lashed out with the twitching blacksnake.

" I beg your pardon! " mimicked the provost marshal. " Captain mama's boy! You'll whine and cry for your mama before we're through with you — "

The color rushed to Nathan's face.

Provost Marshal Cunningham laughed and snapped out an order to the guard. " Throw the cursed pup in the greenhouse and put on a double guard."

What a strange place to spend the last night of his life, Nathan mused, looking about him at the odd, exotic plants that were withering away for want of care since the master of the house had fled before the British. He sat down on a wooden bench, his legs weak. Disconnected pictures flashed through his mind: Abigail, the night the Deacon had brought her home, so pretty and so kind; Alice, in her bright red hood, the day he had gone to Old Jeff's store to meet her; the family sitting in their pew at church, his father all stiffness from his back to his mustaches, the little boys trying so hard to wiggle inconspicuously, little Joanna sighing because her legs were weary from dangling, Elizabeth, with her smooth braids, sitting almost as still and straight as the Deacon; Alice, sitting beside his sick bed only a few short weeks before; Abigail again, grayer and older, looking up from the churn with eyes full of tears when he had told her how much she meant to him and saying, " I'll never forget what you've said, Nathan."

A lump rose in his throat and stuck there. Abigail had always insisted that he was going to do something great in the world. He had hoped that he could do something that would be of some good to mankind. And now this — to die as a spy! How sadly disappointed Abigail would be in him! And Alice, and Enoch, and pa, and Alden, and Tallmadge, and Hillhouse, and Dwight, and Hull! Hull had tried to save him from this journey.

The worst of it was being so terribly alone. He ached to have Alice with him, her hand to cling to, the steady light in her eyes to help him through the long hours till the dawn. The misery of his failure was acute; the stigma attached to the death of a spy, cruel. What would this last blow do to Alice? He knew a moment's black despair; then another picture flashed into his mind and buoyed him up: Alice before the fireplace, that last night of his furlough, saying, " Nathan, the old coat of arms has always meant a great deal to you, hasn't it? " And his own reply, " I've always thought it stood for a very special brand of courage." It was now that he must call up that special courage from somewhere out of the deep heritage of the Hale past.

He did not know how long he had sat without moving on the hard seat in the center of the greenhouse, but it must have been hours. Suddenly he came to himself. He must hurry. The dawn might not be far off, and there were things he must do. He moved stiffly toward the door and spoke to the guard standing inside.

Lost in his black thoughts, he had not been aware of the soldier's presence.

" I wonder if I might have pen and paper," he asked, " and a candle to see by. I'd like to write some letters."

" I'll see what I can do." The guard's voice was kind. He summoned an outside guard. " See if you can get paper and pen and a candle for the prisoner," he said.

" The order has to go to Cunningham," the second guard replied doubtfully.

" I know, but try."

" And a Bible, if you would," Nathan added.

He paced the length of the greenhouse, waiting for the guard to return. He would write to Alice, and his father, and Abigail. He would like to write to Enoch too, and Elizabeth, if he had time. Elizabeth had named her new little son for him.

There was commotion outside the greenhouse, and the coarse, angry voice of Cunningham. The door opened and the provost marshal stormed in, swaying drunkenly, the candle in his hand lurching precariously.

" Where is he? Where is he? " he shouted. " The lousy, white-livered ass. Waking me up in the middle of the night to ask for a Bible! Oh, there you are! What do you think I am, a priest? I'll teach you to wake me up — " The blacksnake came down, but Nathan was too quick for it. He sprang to one side, grabbed the whip from Cunningham's unsteady hand, and handed it to the outside guard.

Cunningham lurched out the door in pursuit of his blacksnake.

" I'm sorry, sir," the guard said, closing the door and turning the key. " He's drunk. And besides, he's a black devil."

" You did your best," Nathan told him. His breath was coming fast. He went back to the rustic bench, dropped to his knees, and prayed.

He was still on his knees when the first dim light began to mold vague forms out of the darkness. The voice of Cunningham fell heavily on the early stillness, his words still thick. Nathan rose and found that his heart was pounding hard and fast.

It was a relief to be led out into the open air. The stars were still visible. He had always loved them. This would be the last time he would see them.

Cunningham was noisily giving orders. Nathan paid no attention to what he said, but he did give heed when a quiet voice broke into Cunningham's bluster.

" Provost Marshal, may I not make your prisoner at ease in my tent until your preparations are completed? " It was Captain Montressor.

Cunningham was too busy to be bothered. " Yes, yes," he sputtered, paying slight attention.

" My tent is right here," Captain Montressor said at Nathan's side. " I think you would be more comfortable waiting there, Captain Hale."

" Thank you," Nathan said, his voice husky with appreciation. It was good to receive a word of kindness when he needed human comfort so badly.

" Is there anything I can do for you? " Montressor asked, when they were inside the tent.

" I should like very much to have pen and paper —

and a Bible," Nathan replied quickly. Perhaps there was still time to write a word to Alice.

" But the chaplain? " Montressor asked in surprise, reaching for writing materials. " Didn't he — "

" I have not seen a chaplain."

Montressor's lips set in a tight line. He handed Nathan paper, pen, and ink, then threw back the lid of his army trunk to find his Bible. " Sit there at the table," he said over his shoulder.

Nathan took up the pen and wrote quickly. His hand was steady. It seemed to him that his mind had never been clearer. Captain Montressor found the Bible and laid it on the table before him. There was no sound in the tent except the even, steady scratching of the pen. Montressor glanced at the light that was growing steadily brighter in the east.

" Is there any passage in the Bible I could find for you? " he asked.

" Yes, if you would, please — the Sermon on the Mount." Nathan did not look up, nor pause.

Montressor turned the pages to the fifth chapter of Matthew and laid the open book on the table. The noise of Nathan's pen stopped abruptly.

" Do you think you could see that these get through the lines for me? " he asked. " One is to my father, and one to my sweetheart."

" Certainly, certainly," Montressor replied, agitation in his voice.

Nathan reached for the Bible, and his eyes ran hungrily over the familiar words: " Blessed are the poor

in spirit: for theirs is the kingdom of heaven. Blessed
are they that mourn: for they shall be comforted. . . .
Blessed are they which are persecuted for righteousness'
sake. . . . I am not come to destroy, but to fulfil."

The stillness in the tent was broken by Cunningham's bellowing approach. He stooped to enter the
tent, then straightened and stood glaring at the scene
before him.

"You — you — " Anger choked him. He snatched
the Bible from Nathan's hand and sent it hurtling to a
far corner. "Readin' the Bible, air ye, ye lousy, white-
livered coward."

Cunningham reached for the letters that lay on the
table. He picked them up, ran his eyes over the pages,
and tore them to bits. The fine pieces of white paper
fell like snow on the cold ground.

Nathan's throat ached. Now they would never know
how he thought of them at the last, how he loved them,
why he had done this thing.

He walked out of the tent and marched up the hill.
His lips moved. "God, make Alice feel the warmth of
my love always. I promised it to her." They entered an
apple orchard at the top of the hill. For a moment
Nathan felt a strange comfort. The sweet, tangy smell
of the ripening fruit brought home very near. Then
he saw the rope dangling from a straight limb of a red-
laden tree, and beside it a ladder.

"Up on the ladder! " Cunningham barked hoarsely.

Nathan obeyed.

"Face front! "

He turned. There was a motley group of curious townspeople below him and a number of redcoats. He did not really see them. There would be no friendly face to whom he could turn, no one who would care. Then his eyes rested on the figure of an officer standing at attention, his face strained, and his eyes full of compassion. It was Montressor. As Nathan's eyes came to rest on the British captain, Montressor raised his hand in a quick salute.

Nathan closed his eyes and prayed as the rope was placed about his neck.

Cunningham's bullying voice, sharp with sarcasm, cut through to his consciousness. " Now, Captain Hale, let's have your dying speech."

That was the bitter moment. What was there to say at the end of a life with which he had hoped to do so much, a life in which no " great things " had been accomplished, a life that was ending ignominiously?

Could he have known that his death was to arouse and inspire the American troops, uniting them as nothing else could have done, the weight of failure would have lifted. Could he have known that he was rendering such a service to his country as he had longed to render, the hour would have been less dark. Could he have known that he was not giving his life in vain — But he did not know.

Suddenly, however, he seemed to see the coat of arms over the fireplace at Coventry. Courage! He straightened his shoulders, lifted his head, and looked out over the crowd below. His voice was clear and firm.

" I only regret that I have but one life to lose for my country."

Cunningham himself kicked out the ladder, and the pink of the dawn — a new dawn for the cause of American independence — went black before Nathan Hale's eyes.